BITTER BRONX

Other Books by Jerome Charyn

FICTION

I Am Abraham
Under the Eye of God
The Secret Life of Emily Dickinson
Johnny One-Eye: A Tale of the American Revolution
The Green Lantern
Hurricane Lady
Captain Kidd
Citizen Sidel
Death of a Tango King
El Bronx
Little Angel Street
Montezuma's Man
Back to Bataan (young adult)
Maria's Girls
Elsinore
The Good Policeman
Paradise Man
War Cries Over Avenue C
Pinocchio's Nose
Panna Maria
Darlin' Bill
The Catfish Man
The Seventh Babe
Secret Isaac
The Franklin Scare
The Education of Patrick Silver
Marilyn the Wild
Blue Eyes
The Tar Baby
Eisenhower, My Eisenhower
American Scrapbook
Going to Jerusalem
The Man Who Grew Younger & Other Stories
On the Darkening Green
Once upon a Droshky

NONFICTION

Joe DiMaggio: The Long Vigil
Marilyn: The Last Goddess
Raised by Wolves: The Turbulent Art and Times of Quentin Tarantino
Savage Shorthand: The Life and Death of Isaac Babel
Gangsters & Gold Diggers: Old New York, the Jazz Age, and the Birth of Broadway
Bronx Boy
Sizzling Chops & Devilish Spins: Ping-Pong and the Art of Staying Alive
The Black Swan
The Dark Lady from Belorusse
Movieland: Hollywood and the Great American Dream Culture
Metropolis: New York as Myth, Marketplace and Magical Land

GRAPHIC NOVELS (WITH FRANÇOIS BOUCQ)

The Magician's Wife
Billy Budd, KGB
Little Tulip (forthcoming)

BRONX

Thirteen Stories

JEROME
CHARYN

LIVERIGHT PUBLISHING CORPORATION
A Division of W. W. Norton & Company
NEW YORK LONDON

Bitter Bronx: Thirteen Stories is a book of short stories. All of the characters, other than those well-recognized public or historical figures whom the reader will readily identify, are products of the author's imagination, and all of the settings, locales, dialogue, and events have been invented by the author or are used fictitiously. In all other respects, any resemblance to actual events, or to real persons, living or dead, is entirely coincidental.

Printed in the United States of America
First Edition

For information about permission to reproduce selections from this book, write to Permissions, Liveright Publishing Corporation, W. W. Norton & Company, Inc., 500 Fifth Avenue, New York, NY 10110

For information about special discounts for bulk purchases, please contact W. W. Norton Special Sales at specialsales@wwnorton.com or 800-233-4830

Manufacturing by Quad Graphics Fairfield
Book design by Helene Berinsky
Production manager: Julia Druskin

Library of Congress Cataloging-in-Publication Data

Charyn, Jerome.
[Short stories. Selections]
Bitter Bronx : thirteen stories / Jerome Charyn. — First edition.
pages ; cm
ISBN 978-0-87140-489-3 (hardcover)
1. Bronx (New York, N.Y.)—Fiction. I. Title.
PS3553.H33A6 2015
813′.54—dc23

2015002080

Liveright Publishing Corporation
W. W. Norton & Company, Inc.
500 Fifth Avenue, New York, N.Y. 10110
www.wwnorton.com

W. W. Norton & Company Ltd.
Castle House, 75/76 Wells Street, London W1T 3QT

1 2 3 4 5 6 7 8 9 0

This book is for Marie-Pierre Bay

ACKNOWLEDGMENTS

These thirteen stories were published in slightly different form in the following magazines and anthologies:

"Lorelei": *The Atlantic,* Fiction 2010.
"Adonis": *The American Scholar,* Winter 2011.
"Archy and Mehitabel": *The American Scholar,* Summer 2012.
"The Cat Lady's Kiss": *StoryQuarterly,* vol. 44, 2010.
"Silk & Silk": *Narrative Magazine,* Story of the Week, 2010–11.
"Little Sister": *The Atlantic,* Fiction 2011.
"Marla": *The Southern Review,* Autumn 2013.
"Dee": *Fiction,* no. 57, 2011.
"Princess Hannah": *Storie,* vol. 57–58, April 2006.
"Milo's Last Chance": *Epoch,* vol. 60, no. 2, 2011.
"Alice's Eyes": *American Short Fiction,* vol. 60, no. 2, 2011.
"Major Leaguer": *Ellery Queen's Mystery Magazine,* September–October, 2013.
"White Trash": *Bronx Noir,* edited by S. J. Rozan. New York: Akashic Books, 2007.

CONTENTS

AUTHOR'S NOTE

For a long time I couldn't go back to the Bronx. It felt like a shriek inside my skull, or a wound that had been stitched over by some insane surgeon, and I didn't dare undo any of the stitches. It was the land of deprivation, a world without books or libraries and museums, where fathers trundled home from some cheese counter or shoe factory where they worked, with a monumental sadness sitting on their shoulders, where mothers counted every nickel at the butcher shop, bargaining with such deep scorn on their faces that their mouths were like ribbons of raw blood, while their children, girls and boys, were instruments of disorder, stealing, biting, bullying whoever they could and whimpering when they had the least little scratch.

I was the only one who had a library card—not that I was any more of a reader than they were, but the library, a good mile from my tenement near Southern Boulevard, was sacred ground. It was one of those limestone palaces Andrew Carnegie had built in the Lower Depths of the Bronx so that the poor could have their own bundle of books to borrow. But I never used my borrower's card, not once. I sat at an enormous oak table, near the library's radiators, and sniffed the curious perfume of books on the shelves with their leather jackets and crumbling, yellow paper—it was, I imagined, the sweet smell of a morgue. Still, I hadn't walked a mile just to breathe in that aroma.

The librarians at this particular Carnegie branch were young and lively and vivacious in the wool sweaters they wore summer and winter. They might have been trainees, performing a kind of "military service" in the outlands. But for some reason I had become their pet—the little silent gypsy in ragged clothes. They fed me from their own lunch boxes on Saturday afternoons, sandwiches with chopped olives and pieces of exotic fruit that were as bulbous and succulent as they were; they all came from a college called Smith, in Massachusetts somewhere, and they yakked about their sweethearts, who weren't doctors and lawyers or even librarians, but plumbers and carpenters in their college town of Northampton. They confided in me as if I were some neutral ghost and not a boy of flesh and blood, just because I ate their olives. They told me about their "love nest," as they called it, at the Hotel Northampton on King Street, since the plumbers and carpenters were married men, you see, with wives and mothers-in-law and a brace of children. They couldn't meet at one of the college cafés on Main Street, and so they practically lived on room service with their beaux. And that's why they were librarians, I learned. It wasn't out of some grand motive to succor the poor. The college had hired some sort of detective, an assistant to an assistant dean who discovered their love nest at the Northampton. And as a kind of penance they enrolled in a makeshift library program; that's how they arrived in the Lower Depths—it was like a year abroad in the Bronx.

I cherished their company, drank Earl Grey with them in the staff closet at the library. They talked about Hermann Hesse and Anaïs Nin, and a novel by Virginia Woolf in which a woman changes into a man. I loved to listen, but wild as I was, I never dreamt of looking for Anaïs Nin on the library shelves. And then

I lost my chance. These Circes from Smith disappeared one afternoon and didn't even have the grace to leave a forwarding address. Perhaps their year of penance was over and they'd gone back to Smith. But the librarians who replaced them were from some forlorn school in the sticks; I could see my own sense of the void in their eyes.

My one solace was to hike halfway across the borough, from Crotona Park to Tremont Avenue, and up Burnside to the Grand Concourse, that mecca of middle-class Jews, and then back to Belmont, where John Garfield, the Bronx's own Clark Gable, had once lived. Meantime, I stopped at one of the mafioso restaurants along Arthur Avenue's restaurant row. I was always welcome there. The owner must have thought I was some bastard child who belonged to one of their own lost princes. He took pity on me, and I sat at a communal table with merchants and underbosses and their blond mistresses, who ate linguine with paper gloves that protected their nail polish.

These were serious eaters; there was very little banter at the table. We all stabbed at the lettuce with our forks from the same gigantic salad bowl. We all dabbed our bread in a dish of olive oil. I couldn't have been more than eleven when this ritual began. But I sipped red wine from a shot glass like everyone else, and my heart began to palpitate after the fifth cup of espresso. That's how I walked home to my tenement near the elevated tracks, with my father caught in his chronic depression, while my mother dipped chocolate on hazelnut paste at the confectioner's factory on Boston Road, my older brother learned the jeweler's art at a vocational high school, and my baby brother barely out of the crib.

I sought escape routes, applied for a special program at the University of Chicago that whisked you out of junior high and put you in a college dorm; I always lamented that I didn't get in. But at least I had my walks up Tremont Avenue. And then all of that changed. Robert Moses, our master builder, believed he could rescue the borough by building a highway right through it. He destroyed entire neighborhoods and dynamited a path right along the Bronx's spine, so that it would be forever divided into north and south, with a no-man's-land on either side of the Cross Bronx Expressway, his monument to himself, and whatever was south of this monument would slowly slip into ruin.

Robert Caro wrote an elegy to East Tremont in *The Power Broker* (1974). By 1965, he said, "apartment buildings that had been so precious to people who had lived in them were ravaged hulks. Windows, glassless except for the jagged edges around their frames, stared out on the street like sightless eyes."

Soon the southern half of the borough would begin to burn, as landlords torched their own buildings to collect whatever insurance they could. And young gang lords performed their own pyrotechnics, as they battled over this desolate turf. But it wasn't these turf wars that kept me out of the Bronx. It was the memory of a prior desolation, a void that clung to my bones. By this time I'd graduated from college and was sort of a hired gun, going from university to university, with the impossible task of teaching students how to write. I lived in Barcelona for a while, wrote a suite of crime novels based on my older brother, who had given up the jeweler's art to become a homicide detective and expert on the Mafia. What held me in his thrall was the crazy wisdom he had, that sense of lawlessness within the law. I could imagine how brutal he had become, like some bitter angel slapping with his left hand.

And then, one day, I went back to the Bronx. I was fifty years old. The BBC was doing a documentary on the Bronx—it must have seemed like an exotic place to the British, with mile upon mile of rubble that reminded them of the London Blitz. We roamed the badlands in a big van, and I felt a kind of exhilaration, as if I inhabited all the empty spaces, and I realized that I had been shaped as a writer not with the words I didn't have, not with lavish pencil cases, not with library books I had never borrowed, but with some ghost's vocabulary. I'd filled that amorphous void of the South Bronx with my own imagination. And as I stood on a hill near the Grand Concourse with the BBC and its camera crew, peering at the carcasses of burnt apartment houses below, I sensed a willful design in all that ruin, could almost hear a chant, a war cry, or perhaps it was a ringing in my ears. Whatever music I have had risen from that bedlam of the Bronx, all the staccato sounds, the syncopation of sadness and loss. I'd been like an amnesiac during my self-banishment from the Bronx, never realizing that each sentence I wrote had come from these Lower Depths.

The Bronx is still "burning"—it has some of the poorest barrios in the whole United States. The Art Deco palaces along the Grand Concourse have been refurbished, but the blight will never really go away. That's not why I wrote these thirteen stories. I'd been riding along the Concourse several years ago when I saw a hand-painted signboard above the entrance of one particular palace:

SAME DAY OCCUPANCY

I could have ended my journey in the middle of the block and moved right in.

And those three words hanging from a bit of string inspired the first story in this collection, "Lorelei." But *Bitter Bronx* is no sentimental journey through my own traces as a child. Diane Arbus' photo *A Jewish giant at home with his parents in the Bronx, N.YC., 1970*, disturbed me from the moment I discovered it in a book of her photographs; I could have been that giant, with his curly hair and his cane, hovering over his tiny, bewildered parents, like some monster of the New World. I wasn't eight feet tall, but I must have bewildered my own parents, who couldn't understand my long silences and wolflike wanderings. And so I decided to write my own Bronx tale about Diane Arbus and her giant.

I was a substitute teacher in the city's public schools for a while, hoping to earn my keep as a writer by teaching once or twice a week while living in a closet in Washington Heights, which was really an outpost of the Bronx. But my plans always went awry. While teaching a few days at the High School of Performing Arts, I learned that the teacher whose classes I had taken over suddenly got very sick, and I was asked to stay on the for the rest of the semester. I got along with the students because I felt like the same sort of neophyte; they were student actors and dancers, and I was a writer who had never published a word. I could have stayed at Performing Arts for the rest of life, "Mr. C.," the sub in baggy pants. But how could I write *and* attend to these students? And so my stories abound with teachers on their own odd journeys—and petty criminals who never left the Bronx, and a wealthy lawyer from Central Park West who lost her little sister somewhere close to the Bronx Botanical Garden. There's also a cat lady—a Latina cashier on Arthur Avenue—who finds herself in love with an Albanian prince. But Robert Moses' highway serves as a not so silent character in these stories, a phantom that crawls between the lines. I couldn't have written this book without that strange man, who never enriched himself, who walked around with holes in his shoes and caused such heartbreak to people in the Bronx, impoverished them and their borough in so many ways.

LORELEI

Howell was still on the lam. He'd been a grifter most of his life, a guy without a permanent address. He had six Social Security cards, seven driver's licenses, a potpourri of voter registration cards, bankbooks under a dozen names. He was Mark Crawford in Florida, Mel Eisenstein in Tennessee. He'd never declared any income, never paid any tax, never been caught. His grift was quite simple. He'd settle into a small town, deposit ten thousand dollars into the local bank, walk around in a very conservative suit, register at the best hotel, and wait: the women would always come to him. He never poked around, never asked questions, never made a list of wealthy widows.

Howell had beautiful hands; that's what the widows noticed first when they stepped onto the porch of the hotel and discovered Howell reading the *Wall Street Journal.* Sometimes they hinted at marriage after a ten-minute talk. Howell avoided spinsters and old maids, who were nervous about money no matter how much they had in the bank. He would have had to have been a bird of prey, a handsome hawk, to pry a bankbook from their fingers. But the widows fell right into his grift. The secret was very simple: they didn't like to live alone. The widows were the real birds of prey. They grasped at Howell with their forceful talons. He could have wreaked havoc on the town had he been some kind of Don Juan. But he always settled on a single widow and shut his eyes to the rest of the field. And it usually wasn't the richest one. The grift depended on how authentic he was. He would only chisel from a widow he might have married. He had to be attracted to the woman, imagine spending his life with her. He couldn't have lasted five minutes with a chatterbox. And when he took her to bed, he wasn't dreaming of his score. The chiseler fell in love, even if only for five minutes. And the widow could feel the tug of his passion.

He didn't discuss money. The widow would bring it up, talk about her holdings, as if to lasso him to her heart. She didn't want him to stray, to find his adventure elsewhere. And then she would be curious about what her new *intended* did. Howell would smile and make love to her again. She'd have to use very tender talons. Couldn't she invest in one of his enterprises? It would tie her to him. And he'd offer her a share of some phantom enterprise at a stingy rate of return, less than she could make on a jumbo certificate at the bank. It was the unattractiveness of what he offered that always drew the widows in. He'd suggest a cautious investment of a few thousand dollars, and she'd write him a check for fifty grand.

Howell didn't disappear with the check. He'd let it sit for a while, have lunch with the widow's daughters and sons, and begin returning bits and pieces of her investment, until she had half of it back, and then he'd close his account and move on. It was Howell's own sense of limits that saved him. Sometimes a widow didn't wake to the chisel for months, and sometimes she never woke to it, having convinced herself that her sweetheart with the beautiful hands would return with the remainder of her capital.

That's why Howell was never caught. He lent a certain grace to his grift, even value to whatever he grabbed. The widows never felt cheated. They remembered the dark-haired stranger who drifted into their lives and made love to them like some Manhattan sheik.

But Howell had little to do with Manhattan. He was from the Bronx. And because of his own odd chivalry, that ceiling he put on whatever he stole, Howell never grew rich.

He was middle-aged, well past fifty, and couldn't bear to romance another widow. A swindler might fall prey to someone else's grift and end up panhandling on South Beach, among all the models and the movie stars. And he couldn't even say what kind of curious radar or homing device had brought him back to the Grand Concourse in his Lincoln Town Car. Howell had little nostalgia in his blood. He was the son of a Bronx superintendent and happened to grow up among all the rich Concourse brats. He inhabited a cellar apartment, with barred windows that gave out onto a backyard and a storage bin for the building's junk. But he'd had a Concourse address, like all the brats. He lived at the Lorelei, an Art Deco apartment palace near Joyce Kilmer Park, on a hill above what was then Yankee Stadium. He could peer right into that enormous horseshoe from the Lorelei's roof, and that's how he watched Yankee games; even with binoculars he couldn't see very much, but he could tell when the Yankees were at bat from the tumult of the crowd. And as a boy up on the roof Howell realized he would never be near enough to what he wanted; he still was "binoculars" away.

And here he was, driving past the Lorelei, when he saw a huge signboard on the front wall:

SAME DAY OCCUPANCY
Superintendent on the Premises

Finding an apartment at the Lorelei had once been impossible; together with the Lewis Morris Apartments, near Mount Eden Avenue, it was the most distinguished address on the Concourse. But the Lewis Morris didn't have Yankee Stadium at its door; the

Lorelei did. And what kind of crazy impulse sent Howell looking for the superintendent, who no longer lived in the cellar, but had a sterling apartment on the ground floor.

Howell didn't care how many apartments were available, or if the first month was free. The super seemed desperate to have him. His name was Nando, and he was from Venezuela.

"I want Apartment 6A," Howell said.

Nando peered at him like an artful poker player. "That's impossible. It's our flagship apartment, the top of the line—with a triple exposure. It's like being on your own planet."

But Howell saw right behind the super's ploy. "You don't have to tell me about 6A. I've played hopscotch on its parquet floors."

Now Nando was alarmed. "Are you some kind of burglar?"

Howell laughed and told him that he'd lived in the Lorelei as a child, that his own father had once had Nando's job.

"Then you know about Miss Naomi?"

Howell froze; he'd tumbled into a secret little game. *Miss Naomi.* She was the reason he'd drifted back to this land of desolation. Naomi Waldman, the little Bronx debutante who'd driven Howell wild when he lived under the ground with his pa. The Waldmans owned the building and two or three other Art Deco palaces along the Grand Concourse. Apartment 6A was their castle keep, the official residence of the Waldmans, where they gave their parties and concert recitals, and where Naomi Waldman, their only child, studied and took private dancing lessons in one of the Lorelei's sultanic rooms. Hugo Waldman was the paterfamilias of the whole tribe—nephews, cousins, and uncles-in-law who lived along the Concourse in lesser palaces. He'd come from Hungary at the age of five, was orphaned at nine, but was still able to attend Harvard and Columbia Law. He'd been a fencing champion at Harvard and he fluttered around on the balls of his feet, like a man who was superior to anyone else in the room.

He went into real estate, eschewed Park Avenue, and established himself in a storefront right on the Grand Concourse. He married one of the local beauties, a myopic girl without much credentials other than her ability to play the violin. Her name was Helena Goldenhagen, and she pleased this young paterfamilias of the Bronx. He bought the Lorelei with the help of a Bronx savings bank, had Helena give recitals at home. She played in front of the Concourse's little kings—councilmen, department store moguls, savings bank scions, even the borough president.

She gave birth to Naomi between two recitals. She was twenty-seven years old. Carrying Naomi in her womb had dazed Helena, left her with some kind of permanent squint, as if her insides had been seared. The child was born in its own bullet of blood. Helena stopped playing the violin. She couldn't nurse Naomi. They had to call in an Armenian woman with her own supply of milk. This woman suckled the child. She had a mustache that Helena couldn't bear. Hugo had to fire the wet nurse.

But it didn't harm Naomi, who burst out of her baby clothes. It was 1950, a decade before the Grand Concourse began to decline. Hugo would lope along the Concourse with his daughter on his back—the entire boulevard her domain. She was incorrigible by the time she was three, throwing tantrums and hissing at her nurses and Helena, who had already withdrawn to the back rooms of the family's apartment-castle. Even Hugo could hardly keep up with a little dark-haired tyke who never ceased to explore. And that's how Howell was first introduced to Naomi Waldman.

Oh, he'd seen her before, wrapped in scarves, coming out of her father's Lincoln. But *his* father had told him to keep away from Mr. Hugo and the Little Miss. Howell didn't have much to do with the building or its magnificent lobby of hammered silver and black marble that shone like devilish, blinding glass. He entered the building through a gate that led right into its bowels, and that's where he remained, unless he was at school, or was ordered by his pa to polish the black marble in the lobby.

He must have been six or seven that first time, and the Little Miss was about the same age. She was already wearing lipstick. She'd come from a school play. She looked like a witch in her mascara. She'd gone into the super's apartment without even knocking on the door. Howell lived alone with his pa. His mother had run away with another man before Howell was five. This devil of a man had something to do with Mr. Hugo. He was a dentist who had an office in the building—his teeth were capped with silver. Howell recalled those silver teeth. He didn't have much of a recollection of his mother. She had arms that moved like magical sticks. Her hair smelled of silk. But he couldn't have told you the color of her eyes, or how tall she was.

His encounter with Naomi was much more vivid. She'd come to him in high heels, a girl of six or seven who seemed to walk on stilts. She'd already appropriated her mother's squint.

"I beg your pardon," she sang in a voice sweet as a violin. "I must have strayed. Might I trouble you for a cup of water?"

Howell rushed over to the sink. And she followed him into the kitchen like a pony on high heels. He had to rinse his own drinking cup and wait until the water ran cold in the faucet. He held the dented tin up like a chalice and handed it to Naomi.

"Do you have a biscuit?" she asked. "I'm famished."

Howell was bewitched. He couldn't have known that Naomi had gone to elocution school and had been taught to speak like a little duchess in her own manor house. The voices he heard in the Bronx never had Naomi's lilt. Even Mr. Hugo, who'd had his own fencing master at Harvard, spoke with the usual Bronx burl—it was gangster talk, though Howell hadn't met many gangsters on the Grand Concourse.

He had the devil of a time coming up with a biscuit for Naomi. All he could find was a stale soda cracker in one of the tins his mother had left behind when she ran off with the dentist. He let her feast on the cracker with strawberry jam.

And that's when his pa appeared with Mr. Hugo. Pa's eyes had narrowed down to pale blue slits. All the usual paranoia had settled in. That's why his mother had abandoned this cave under the Lorelei. She couldn't bear the darkness *and* his pa's paranoia. But why did she leave Howell behind with her own little gallery of tin boxes?

Mr. Hugo wasn't suspicious at all. He had a razor-sharp mustache, like Smilin' Jack, Howell's favorite character in the funny papers. All Mr. Hugo needed was a pair of goggles and an aviator's cap and he could have been Jack.

Pa twisted Howell's ear in front of Naomi and Mr. Hugo. "Carlton," he grumbled, "why are you bothering Mr. Hugo's little girl?"

No one called him Carlton, except his pa. Even his teachers at elementary school learned to call him Howell. And he felt ashamed in front of the little duchess. But she rescued him right away.

"Super," she said, with little blinks of mascara, "your boy was most helpful to me. I was lost in this underground passageway, looking for the bin where all the travelers' trunks are stored. And Carl fed me a scrumptious biscuit and a cup of water."

"Was he a gentleman with you?" asked his pa, one of his pale eyes practically screwed out of its socket.

"A perfect gentleman," she said. "I was playing Scarlett O'Hara in my elocution class, and I ran all the way home in my costume."

The little duchess offered Pa her hand to kiss. He was trembling, but he pecked her hand with his lips, while she winked at Howell. Then she and Mr. Hugo crept back into that shadowland under the building. Pa waited ten minutes before he beat Howell with his belt buckle, just for offering a soda cracker to the little duchess.

That was fifty years ago, but it stuck in Howell's memory like a strange claw. He couldn't believe that "Miss Naomi" could still be found in 6A. How could the Waldmans have remained at the Lorelei while the Concourse slid into oblivion? Howell had left home while the Cross Bronx Expressway was being built. It was tunneled right under the Concourse near Mount Eden, in some marvel of engineering, but it still cut the Concourse in two and created desolation on both sides of its path. The Bronx now had a series of ghost neighborhoods, with concrete walls and concrete gardens. But Howell was gone before the Bronx began to burn and wild dogs roamed Claremont Park. He had to leave once his father could no longer seize him by the ear. Howell had grown too tall. He vanished without a note, before he ever had a chance to murder his pa.

Mr. Hugo had always been kind to him, had given him pocket money to accomplish little household chores. He'd shellac the desk in Naomi's room, repair a chipped tile, take Helena for walks in Joyce Kilmer Park. He'd learned all the skills and handicrafts of a superintendent's boy. He'd also become Naomi's slave and part-time beggarly brother. He was forever in her room, which was as large as the grand salon at the Concourse Plaza. She could never find a wardrobe that fit. She'd burst out of her clothes from season to season. She was voluptuous at thirteen, and it was almost as if she vampirized whatever small charms Helena had left. Her mother began to shrivel, while Naomi swayed like a tigress. She had marriage proposals before she was fifteen. Millionaires pursued Naomi for their sons; and sometimes for themselves.

It was Howell's misfortune that he had to listen to all their clatter. Bankers wanted to elope with her, realtors wanted to buy her a building. But Mr. Hugo had flooded her mind with a sense of Grand Concourse culture. Why would she need a building when she had her own grand salon? While her miraculous chest fluttered and her calves swelled, she dreamt of marrying a Bronx Van Gogh.

"Carl," she told him, "you can't have art without suffering."

She was the only one who was allowed to call him Carl. And he was obliged to commiserate with her. Since she was constantly chauffeured from class to class, and went to school with the heir to this fortune or that, it was difficult for her to meet struggling artists and musicians. And she had no ambition to venture outside the Bronx. Howell would escort her to the Loew's Paradise or the Botanical Garden, with little envelopes of cash Mr. Hugo stuffed into his pocket. He'd clutch her hand at the movies whenever a monster was on the screen. But he could never have become Van Gogh.

And yet one afternoon, while they were in the dark of the Loew's Paradise, with its Alhambra walls and star-crusted ceiling, Howell's hand strayed upon her breast. How could he ever have described her heaving heart? She didn't brush his hand away. It was the most insanely erotic moment of Howell's life.

Nothing was the same after that. They would stumble about on the queen-sized sofa in her room, neither of them really knowing what to do. And then, after a few such fumblings, she wiggled out of her clothes and lay with Howell in her panties and bra, as if both of them had been entombed. Helena found them like that and started to shriek.

Howell had to sit in the hall like a prisoner until Mr. Hugo arrived. His mustache barely bristled. He seemed disappointed in Howell.

"You can't marry my little girl," he said. "Not because you're the super's boy. I've always liked you, but I don't fancy you as my son-in-law." Howell was fifteen at the time. "You'll never have an artistic career, and Naomi would die without culture."

Howell packed whatever little he had, got on a Greyhound, and had been wandering ever since. He'd had a hundred different jobs until he discovered his own particular way with women. He'd never been rich, but it didn't really matter. He wanted no permanent attachments.

Now he was back where he started, and *his* Yankee Stadium sat like a feeble, gutted ghost beside the new stadium. But what irked him wasn't a green graveyard at the bottom of the hill. It was that other ghost out of his childhood.

"Nando, what is Miss Naomi doing in 6A?"

"She never left. She's been sittin' up there since the day she was born."

"Even when the crackheads ruled this part of the Bronx?"

Nando sneered at him. "We never had crack at the Lorelei. Mr. Hugo still owns the building. He and Miss Naomi gotta eat."

"Did the Little Miss ever marry?"

She had many suitors, Nando said. "She was a real ball breaker." She had invitations to Italy, cruises along the Nile. The finest Manhattan chefs were chauffeured uptown to give her private cooking classes. But she had no one to test her new palette on except her own papa. And so she prepared candlelight suppers near the Lorelei's wrap-around windows that looked out onto the ravaged heartland of the Bronx. And after all her tutors, and all the little tasks, she ended up in Mr. Hugo's office, as some sort of executive secretary.

She was ravishing in her tailored jackets and argyle socks. But a hardness appeared at the edge of her mouth. She looked at you with eyes that were like tin telescopes. Her voice turned shrill. She began to lose her hair. She herself managed several of her father's apartment houses. She would show up in a hard hat, like some truculent crusader. Soon she was limping, and then she couldn't walk at all. Specialists from Mount Sinai examined her for six months. She was confined to a wheelchair when she was forty. And she had sat and sat on that aluminum throne ever since.

Mr. Hugo was ninety, but he still hopped around on the balls of his feet, like that fencer out of Harvard. He still went to work, still made deals, when he wasn't gallivanting with Naomi in her wheelchair.

Howell picked up whatever furniture he needed at a Bronx fire sale. No sheriff in Louisiana or spurned widow could ever have tracked him to the Lorelei. He lived directly below the Waldmans, in a kind of squirrel's retreat. All his life he'd lived like a squirrel, moving from one retreat to the next.

He found a note on his kitchen table. It was a dinner invitation for that very night, in a childish scrawl.

Dearest Carl, Welcome Home
Dinner at Seven
(We Eat Early in the Bronx)
Apartment 6A

It wasn't even signed, or perhaps "6A" was enough of a signature. He searched for a flower shop and a local winery and found none. He had to invade Manhattan in his Town Car for a white rose and a decent bottle of wine. He wore his best suit, with a paisley tie and a black-on-black shirt.

Mr. Hugo met him at the door. He was also wearing a black shirt.

"My protégé," he said.

Howell liked to introduce himself with a bottle of Château Mouton Rothschild. The name intrigued him. He was certain it couldn't be found in the Bronx.

The little duchess sat on her aluminum throne at the dinner table, in the wondrous light of a candle. She had aged, certainly, and could have been puffed with cortisone, but she had on the same lipstick she wore at seven, the same red smear, when she was the Scarlett O'Hara of her elocution class. He offered her the white rose.

"Carlton," she said, never even bothering to shake his hand, "that's rather daring of you." Her voice had the same old fiddler's ring. That sound fired up his loins. He was her prisoner after a single sentence.

"Honey," Mr. Hugo said. "Don't talk in riddles. You'll scare Howell away."

"But it's not a riddle, Papa," she said, thrusting the rose into her hair, with its thorns. "The white rose is the symbol of love as everlasting war."

Smilin' Jack scratched his mustache and stared at his daughter. "That sounds a little like real estate . . . and we have nothing to sell Howell."

"We have plenty to sell, Papa," she said, while the old man used his corkscrew as some kind of tourniquet to suck that cork right out of the bottle of Bordeaux.

"And what are we selling tonight?"

"Me," the little duchess said.

The old man sat down and started to pour the wine.

"Papa, you'll cause a scandal. You have to let that bottle breathe."

She lurched in her wheelchair and took the bottle out of her father's hand.

"Sit," she said to Howell. "And take off that tie. I can't really bargain while my suitor's wearing such an elegant rag."

Howell laughed deep within his throat and shucked off his paisley tie. A few more minutes of her patter and he would have given all his bank accounts away.

She was the one who served the salad, who raced into the kitchen and raced back in her wheelchair. The old man never moved from the table. Naomi poured the wine after twirling the cork once or twice.

"Papa," she said, wiping some salad oil from her mouth. "You shouldn't have broken our courtship."

"I didn't," he groaned.

"I might have married Carl."

"You were thirteen—a child. Isn't that right, Howell?"

"Fifteen," she said. "With Bronx millionaires breathing down my back. I wanted Carlton."

"But he was the super's boy. He couldn't even play the fiddle."

"He would have fiddled with me."

She served the baked potatoes and the salmon steaks in their tinfoil. She refilled her father's glass.

"If you had really loved me, you would have taken Carl in as a junior partner."

"People would have laughed at me . . . a cellar rat selling real estate."

She swiped her father's cheek, softly, with her silk napkin, but it was the same as a slap.

"You were jealous of him," she said. Then she turned on Howell. "Look at you. You never even crawled out from under my father's shadow. A pair of Smilin' Jacks."

Howell was in misery. She'd robbed him of whatever little thunder he had left.

"Well," she said, "you brought the white rose. What does it mean?"

"Love as everlasting war."

"Didn't I tell you?" she said, rocking in her aluminum throne.

"Miss Naomi, I never loved another living soul."

"And how long have I been waiting, huh, Carl?"

"As long as it took me to crisscross the country a dozen times, romancing widows and a couple of old maids who couldn't even hold a candle to you, swindling them out of a little of their life savings . . ."

"Well, I'm the oldest maid you've ever met. Why haven't you swindled me?"

Suddenly Howell was getting into the hang of talking to this hellion in a wheelchair. All her elocution lessons were just a mask. She was a chiseler from the day she was born.

"I think I'm the one who was swindled, miss. . . . You knew all along the hold you had on me."

"And what if I did?"

"You sent me howling into the wind. I'm lucky to be all in one piece."

Her face softened. She didn't have the same hard curl at the edge of her mouth. Her eyes bled the viscous color of tears.

"But you never wrote me once. You had my address. You didn't even send me a postcard from Arkansas. I had to have my revenge."

"Wait a minute," Mr. Hugo said. "This is taking a bad turn."

And now she wheeled her aluminum throne toward her father with a cold fury.

"Stay out of it, Papa."

They had pears in white wine, with a piece of fruitcake. Mr. Hugo didn't look up from his plate.

"Carl, I've only been with one man in my life, and that's you."

The slice of fruitcake crumbled in Howell's hand.

"I'm going crazy," the old man said, banging his temples with his fists.

"Carl," she sang, "should I tell you a secret? He pays his own daughter to hug him at night. He can't bear to be alone. I wouldn't let him touch me with those claws of his. I wouldn't let him have a single kiss."

She prepared the cups of demitasse. Meanwhile, her father began to shiver and cry. The little duchess tossed a tiny silver spoon at him and he stopped whimpering, but Howell bit right into the lip of his demitasse cup. He'd learned to chisel from these two. They were his teachers. He'd gone on the road with their sounds and smells inside him. His elocution had come from the little duchess, and his dancing swagger from this Smilin' Jack of the West Bronx. He couldn't stay at the Lorelei, or he would be sucked into this team of chiselers. They would swallow him alive.

He folded his napkin and set it on the table, as a child might do. And then he danced out of that apartment-castle on the balls of his feet. They were so occupied in the business of themselves that they didn't even know he was gone.

Howell left his fire-sale furniture for the super. He'd never even signed a lease. Perhaps nobody signed leases at the Lorelei. He had his passport and his bankbooks in the back pocket of his pants. Howell had never been abroad, and had crossed only once from El Paso to Juárez, just to see what it was like. All he found were wild dogs with dust on them and twelve-year-old whores. But a passport lent him some distinction, made him appear like a world traveler to the widows of Kansas and South Dakota.

He crept into his Town Car with a tiny suitcase and the shirt on his back. He was shivering in July. And he lit out from the Grand Concourse with his toe to the floor. Howell was running for his life.

ADONIS

I was fifteen when Rosenzweig discovered me at the Frick Collection. We were both standing in front of Rembrandt's *Polish Rider*, and he came up to me like Count Dracula bathed in perfume and said, "Young man, have you ever modeled before?"

Some nabob with a boutonniere was always trying to flirt with me at the Frick. But Rosenzweig was all business.

"I'm a freshman at the High School of Music and Art," I said.

He handed me his card, said his chauffeur would pick me up after class.

"I wouldn't want a young gentleman such as yourself to miss a day of school, even if it might make him rich."

And then he was gone with that bloodless look of his, like a man made of whitewash. There was a limo waiting for me after class on Monday. We rode down off St. Nicholas Terrace, away from the gargoyles of Music and Art, and into the heart of Manhattan. Rosenzweig & Co. was the Cadillac of clothing cataloguers at the time, occupying a manufacturer's loft near the tiny synagogue for tailors at the corner of Thirty-sixth. It was like having an assault team on a single floor—with showrooms, a printing press, photography studios, and a rat's maze of little offices where Rosenzweig's proofreaders and editors worked from dawn to dusk to spit out catalogues according to his own brutal clock.

The racket was relentless; I fell right into the deafening roar.

I had never seen such a hub of activity, with male and female models prancing about half-undressed. I had a terrible omen the minute after entering Rosenzweig's world of frosted glass. I recognized one of his models—Beth Bacharach, the Bronx bombshell who had dropped out of junior high last year and vanished from our streets. We assumed Beth had either been knocked up or kidnapped, and here she was on Seventh Avenue, modeling brassieres. She couldn't have been much older than sixteen, but she had the dazed look of someone who was mortally wounded. She didn't even glance up when I said hello.

I should have taken Beth with me and run from Rosenzweig, but I walked right into that labyrinth and was photographed wearing a muscle tee-shirt. I blame Marlon Brando. He had worn a muscle tee in *The Men*, playing a paraplegic with biceps bigger than ostrich eggs, and suddenly haberdashers all over town had tee-shirts in their windows instead of bow ties. The photographer, called Gabe, stood behind his tripod with a little black cloth over his head. He couldn't stop muttering to himself.

"The cheekbones, the cheekbones—finally we have our Tartar look."

I was hired on the spot, before they had the chance to gaze into the developer. Rosenzweig and his accountant told me not to worry about working papers. I would be paid off the books, but I wasn't supposed to utter a word to my teachers at Music and Art. I would never have to skip a class or ride the subway at night; a limo would carry me door to door. Of course I suffered. I was an art student who dreamt of Gauguin's tropical sun and Van Gogh's missing ear. I had no time to paint. I had to read *Hamlet* after midnight, in the limousine, under the glare of a shivering lamp. But I had two hundred dollars in my pocket every week—it was 1953, and we were in the middle of a recession. My father hadn't worked in years. He'd fallen into his own dark time. My kid brother was too young to shine shoes. My mother was blind in one eye and losing her sight in the other. I was our sole support.

I didn't wear as many muscle tee-shirts after the Brando mania began to fade. I modeled turtlenecks, bow ties, sport coats, vinyl jackets, or whatever leapt into the national clothing craze. I never saw Beth Bacharach again, and I wondered if she was on the scrap heap of worn-down Rosenzweig models.

Needless to say, I lived in the "narrow" of a schoolbook and the blinking eye of a camera. But I did have one friend, also a freshman at M&A. Miles Neversink. He was a runt, and I would protect him from certain seniors, who might have preyed upon Miles, except that I was tall for my age and had the Tartar cheeks of Rembrandt's Polish Rider—I would return to that portrait at the Frick whenever I had the chance, since it was like looking at some ancestor of mine, with his quiver of arrows and his riding crop.

Miles' dad, Arthur Neversink, was the most celebrated criminal lawyer in Manhattan; a menace in open court, he could flay any government witness, but he couldn't keep Frank Costello out of jail. Prosecutors were still frightened of Arthur. And policemen waved to him whenever they saw his silky white hair. There were rumors that he'd once been a taxi dancer in Hell's Kitchen and that Costello himself had sent him through law school. But I also heard that he'd grown up on the Grand Concourse, that his father had been one of the most prominent manufacturers on Seventh Avenue. I suspect he didn't need Frank Costello's largesse to finance his legal career.

He lived in one of those Art Deco palaces on Central Park West with gangsters and Jewish millionaires who had been shunned by all the palaces on Fifth Avenue and now formed their own incredible clique. They were the new lords of Manhattan. Much of the West Side was still a slum, but they had their golden mile across the street from the park. And there were no muggers or highwaymen along this golden mile. Not because of the police. Frank Costello lived in the same Art Deco palace as Arthur Neversink, lived there on his short furloughs from jail.

That building would soon become my second home. On some evenings I was driven directly from Rosenzweig's Seventh Avenue fortress to the Neversinks on Central Park West; it saved a long trip back to the Bronx. Even when I arrived well after midnight, the Neversinks weren't asleep. There were dinner parties every evening. The main attraction wasn't the mob lawyer himself, but Mrs. Neversink. *Miranda*. She must have been in her mid-thirties at the time. She had sultry gray eyes that seemed to beckon you onto her own private moon. Her hair was slightly unkempt. She always wore a man's shirt and slacks that had never seen an ironing board.

She was a patroness of the arts. That might not have impressed most people, but it had a magical soupçon for a boy who studied painting and lived in the shadow of Vincent van Gogh and his avatar from Wyoming, Jackson Pollock. She had plenty of Pollocks on her walls. She'd sat with him at the Cedar Tavern, shared his little cigars, long before he was known. Miranda had given him pocket money, and Arthur had helped him out of legal scrapes, since Pollock constantly got into fights during his Cedar Tavern days, pulling women's hair, battling with bartenders, as I imagined Van Gogh would have done had he lived in the twentieth century.

I never saw Pollock at the Neversinks' dinner parties. I only saw his paintings, with their lashing rhythm, as if colors could cry out—I would close my eyes and crash right into those time bombs on the wall. And then Miranda would pull me right back into her own terrain. Her musk was enough to make me sick with excitement. I was crazy about her men's shirts. I wish she could have modeled them in Rosenzweig's catalogues. That Seventh Avenue Dracula would have made a killing.

Miranda cursed like a longshoreman. It didn't come from her husband's gangster clients. It was from having been the companion to a band of rogue painters—Pollock, Rothko, de Kooning, Kline—the new gangsters of American art. Her pale eyes would be puffed out whenever I returned from Rosenzweig's after midnight. She would begin to sway.

"Kid, didn't I see you somewhere?"

I was bewildered. I thought she hadn't recognized me in her alcoholic haze. "I go to school with your son," I said.

"No, no, not that," she muttered. "I've seen your face—Arthur, isn't he a handsome boy? My Adonis."

She didn't mean Joey Adonis, Costello's partner in crime, who was looking after business while Costello was in the clink. She meant that minor god who was born with such hot looks he had to spend half the year with Persephone, queen of the underworld, or he would have been seduced by every goddess in ancient Greece.

Miranda must have had Persephone's prescience. A week later I was listed in Rosenzweig's catalogue as "Adonis." I had a page to myself, posing in jockey shorts and muscle tee-shirts with a brooding look. It seems Count Dracula had a lucrative sideline as a pornographer and a pimp. He sold shots of me to wealthy war widows, that is, women who had lost their husbands during World War II. He offered me a hundred-dollar bonus if I'd have dinner with one of these war widows.

I also graduated from the photography studio to the showrooms and the salons, where I could prance around on a platform in my muscle tee-shirt, under the same blinding lights. I wasn't allowed to wash up or change my clothes after these performances. Rosenzweig would slick back my hair, as if he were grooming a prize pony, and with a plum-colored velvet jacket over my muscle tee-shirt, I would climb into the limo, where a war widow was waiting. There was nothing sordid about these assignations.

I would have dinner with the war widows in a rear booth at a northern Italian restaurant on Ninth Avenue. I later realized that the restaurant was owned by Frank Costello, and that these widows had lost their husbands in some gangland version of World War II. They might hold my hand at dinner, but nothing more than that. They were all stunners in their thirties and forties who weren't permitted to marry again, according to some unwritten rule of gangland lore. These widows "slept" in the coffins of their slain husbands.

They couldn't work, but they could go back to school. The widows were as hungry to learn as hawks. I told them about Jackson Pollock, how he lived in the dizzying uncertitude of his art, how his explosion of splotches on canvas was Pollock's own avalanche of pain.

We drank wine that arrived in a cradle and cost a hundred dollars a pop, even if I was too young to drink. We ate chopped salads in silver bowls, broccoli brushed with burning olive oil, glazed carrots, goat cheese, and a hazelnut cake cut into two leaning towers, while we sipped coffee with a *tinto*—stain—of hot milk.

One of the war widows grew impulsive and kissed me on the mouth while we were in the limousine. She begged me to take off my muscle tee-shirt. I did. She brushed my body with her fingers as a blind woman might have done, memorizing the details of my skin. She dug one hand under my belt and caressed the hair on my belly. Then she started to whimper.

"You mustn't think I am wicked," she said. "But it's been so long, and I have forgotten how a man feels. . . . You won't tattle on me, will you, my darling Adonis? They'll lock me up for a month."

I stroked her cheek, and she leapt back like a startled deer.

"You mustn't," she said, "or I'll explode like Mr. Pollock."

Her name was Louise. I never saw her again. I hate to think

that Frank Costello punished her from his federal prison in Pennsylvania. But it was all very confusing to me. I'd become a little whore for the mob; I'm fairly certain that Costello or Joey Adonis had an interest in Rosenzweig's catalogue company. But as Rosenzweig himself had predicted in front of *The Polish Rider*, I was getting rich.

Bankbooks leave a trail, according to Rosenzweig, so I kept my cash in a shoebox under my bed. In the Bronx, circa 1953, we paid our bills with money orders. And because I was busy day and night and my mother was half-blind, and my father too forlorn to be much of a courier, the burden fell on my kid brother, who was nine. He had to dole out cash to the landlord and buy money orders at the savings bank. Soon he was my surrogate.

But the Adonis of Seventh Avenue was falling apart. I could wing it at school, and I didn't mind modeling under the lights, or having my own page in the catalogue. It was the monkey business in the limousine, that powerful eroticism of touch and no touch. I'd grown fond of the war widows and their sad tale of being buried alive. I gobbled up their sadness until it became mine. Miranda must have sensed my inky disposition, and she tried to pull me out of my own skin. She was having a shindig, a gala for indigent artists, and she wanted the two of us, Miles and me, to help her make and serve the hors d'oeuvres.

The shindig was set for that Saturday night, and so I feigned illness and begged off work at Rosenzweig's. I didn't want to sit in a limousine with another war widow, dine in a secret alcove at Villa ——, burn my lips on coffee stained with scalding milk. I spent the whole of Saturday afternoon with Miranda and Miles. First we had lunch on her balcony—smoked salmon on bread roasted in her oven—while we looked upon the greensward of Central Park, with its lake that was like a lopsided heart, and at the alien world of Fifth Avenue. We belonged to that clan of West

Siders who never wore watch fobs or attended debutante balls. We had galas for indigent artists.

It was the most splendid afternoon I'd ever had, preparing hors d'oeuvres with Miranda and Miles. Miranda told me a little about her life. She had come to Manhattan with her parents from the Dominican Republic when she was twelve, had lived on the Upper West Side, where she played ping-pong and chess and attended Joan of Arc Junior High, which had more geniuses per square foot than any other school in America—scientists, writers, artists, musicians, theologians, rabbinical scholars.

"Miranda, did you go to Music and Art?"

And suddenly there was a look on Miranda akin to Pollock, as if she were privy to a hundred little explosions under that beautiful mask of a face. Why did I think of Beth Bacharach, the bombshell who had disappeared from the Bronx? But Miranda wasn't Beth. Miranda could recover from whatever wound she had.

"I wasn't lucky," she said. "My *papi* died. I had to go to work. I quit high school." Now she smiled, with only a hint of Pollock's pain. "It *was* Music and Art. Where else would I have gone? A Latin bagel baby. The school had opened that year—our castle on a Hundred and Thirty-fifth. None of the painting studios were ready. We walked around in all the debris. We had to set up our easels in the hallways. I loved it, that wonderful reek of turpentine. I left in the middle of my second year. The counselors all cried. They worried about what would happen to their bagel baby. But she survived. Look at this! A palace over Central Park. Two gorgeous boys."

She hugged Miles and me, tousled our hair. And we helped her glaze the cupcakes; we rinsed the cherry tomatoes, chopped cucumbers for the gazpacho, put Gouda and shreds of smoked salmon on the crackers, chilled the white wine. Miranda went to fix herself. And when she came back, she wasn't wearing a man's shirt—she was Persephone in a black dress. All the pluck had gone out of me when I saw that black silk cling to Miranda, her bared shoulders like two soft wings, while her arms moved with the dexterity of a magician's uncoiling sticks.

I didn't know any of Miranda's indigent artists—I hadn't struggled enough in any craft to call myself indigent. I couldn't lash out with a rhythm of my own. I had none. My canvases looked like explosions of porridge. But I served Miranda's hors d'oeuvres. Then the doorbell rang, and there was Count Dracula. He was startled to see me. And I was no less startled. But it all made sense, particularly if Frank Costello was financing the catalogue business and wanted an occasional Adonis for his war widows.

"Little one, I thought you were in the Bronx nursing a cold. And what's your connection with Madame Neversink?"

Before I could utter a word, Miranda whisked me away.

"He's poison," she said. "I don't want you to have anything to do with that guy. He's my husband's partner. I never invited him here."

But how could I avoid Rosenzweig? My livelihood depended on him. We would have been on welfare without his catalogue company. And when I caught him whispering in Miranda's ear, I teased out the connection between Rosenzweig and her. That's where she'd gone after a year and a half at M&A—into Dracula's catalogue. She must have modeled brassieres, like Beth, and graduated to the showrooms, which meant dinner dates with manufacturers and mobsters who muscled out other cataloguers, and a bit of syncopated prostitution under Seventh Avenue's veil.

And that's when Arthur entered the story, as Frank Costello's man. It wasn't so hard to imagine. Call it 1938, and Frank Costello is the crime lord of Manhattan, with a finger in every racket, including Rosenzweig & Co. He asks his lawyer to check things out on Seventh Avenue, *Shmatahland.* Arthur saunters into the showroom, expects to find a bimbo in leopard-skin slacks, and discovers Miranda instead. She's eighteen and bored to death with the whole business of modeling, of having to wrestle with mobsters in midtown hotels. And he has to make a very quick calculation. He recognizes the burn of intelligence in her eyes, and her beauty, defiant and timid at the same time. Either he grabs her away from this street of rags or he'll lose her to some manufacturer. He proposes on the spot.

She smiles at him. "Mr. Neversink, we haven't even met."

"Makes no difference," he says.

"What if I can't come up to your expectations?"

"Then I'll suffer," he says.

As a wedding present, their Uncle Frank offers them a duplex in his own West Side apartment-palace. Costello has been fuming. He can't even rent a closet on Fifth Avenue. His long beak isn't welcome there. He plans to wage war against Fifth Avenue, kidnap doormen, set canopies on fire. Arthur has to talk him out of it. "They'll win, Mr. Frank."

"How?" asks the king of crime. "Arthur boy, they don't got the muscle."

"But they have something else—tradition. They have created their own invisible wall. Try to breach that wall, and your whole gang will disappear. They tolerate us, Mr. Frank, as long as we destroy *our* precincts. Enter theirs, and we'll all strangle to death."

"Ah," said Costello. "My Einstein, who keeps me from getting strangled."

And the king went off into his galaxy of crime, far from Fifth Avenue, while Arthur prospered and Miranda gave birth to Miles. He kept returning to Rosenzweig's showrooms, looking for whores, while Miranda gravitated to the Cedar Tavern. She ran with Pollock, became Rothko's muse. That much I would learn from Miranda. She was still in love with her errant mob lawyer, who had proposed to her before she could catch her breath and figure out who the hell he was, and she still had a fondness for Uncle Frank, who would send her a dozen roses on her birthday and continue to plan his assault on Fifth Avenue.

I slid deeper and deeper after that shindig. I didn't mind slaving for Rosenzweig and Frank Costello. I just couldn't bear the cloistered lives of those war widows. Why didn't they rebel, flee from their coffins? But there wasn't a trace of rebellion in their bones. I'd become the doll they could dine with and fondle in the back seat of a limousine. I soaked up more and more of their sadness, the suicidal indifference to their own fate. I faltered at school. I could scratch out compositions under that rattling lamp of the limo, but I was frozen in my studio classes. I couldn't paint. I'd lost my belief in Van Gogh's missing ear—it seemed like madness, not the mystery of great art.

I still had a mountain of cash under my bed. My strutting in the showroom, on Rosenzweig's little runway, had pushed us out of poverty. But I, and not Miranda, was Beth's secret accomplice. I had inherited her mortally wounded look.

And one afternoon, while I was on Rosenzweig's runway, under the sweltering lights, I heard a ruckus. I thought the cops had come to take revenge on Costello and all his enterprises for having dared to covet Fifth Avenue. But it wasn't the cops. It was Miranda in her man's shirt. She ripped out the wiring of the lamps; glass splintered on the floor; bulbs shattered. I listened to Rosenzweig rant and roar.

"Darling, you could go to jail. Mr. Frank won't take kindly to this."

"And you," she said, "shouldn't have a high school student become your whore."

I emptied out the little locker I had at Rosenzweig's, with all my schoolbooks, and then Miranda drove me uptown in her Lincoln Continental. She wasn't addicted to chauffeurs. She preferred her own saddle, she said. But she drove like a wild woman, weaving through traffic, cursing at cab drivers. She started to laugh—and cry.

"Aren't we a pair, kiddo? Two whores on the lam."

And that's when she told me about her former life at Rosenzweig & Co. The manufacturers who danced with her like drunken bears while she fell asleep in their arms, the mobster who couldn't make love until she strapped him into a corset . . .

"But Miranda, you could have worked in a linen shop."

"Kiddo, it would have come to the same thing—customers ogling me and bosses patting my derriere. I was available meat until Arthur happened along, pretending to be the big bad wolf. He swept me right out of Rosenzweig's rooms."

"The way you did with me."

"Didn't I tell you? A couple of whores on the lam."

We roared up the West Side, went into a coffee shop on Ninety-fifth, near Joan of Arc. It was one of those Manhattan sugar bowls where schoolkids spent half their lives. But it didn't jump at night, even with a jukebox. This sugar bowl was a somber place, with darkened booths and sinister coat hangers shaped like hatchets and bulls' horns.

"I lost my cherry in one of those booths," she said. "I was a precocious kid."

I couldn't quell my own curiosity. "Who was the culprit?"

"My art teacher at M&A. He lived across the street with his wife and three girls. He was the neighborhood Gauguin. He was going to abandon his wife and run to Mazatlán with his canvas stretcher and me. . . . He's still wallowing on Ninety-fifth."

Both of us had lime rickeys. You have to nurse a limey rickey along until the syrup begins to settle, and you have to sip it from a straw, or you'll never get that delicious sting. Miranda and I made out a little. It was nothing serious. She was in love with her Concourse lawyer, and I was one more Adonis who happened to be her son's best friend. But I did taste the tartness on her tongue.

She found me a job at a haberdasher's on Broadway. I was the local celebrity, because the other salesclerks recognized my picture in Rosenzweig's catalogue. But my celebrity soon wore thin as we had to compete for sales. They were sharks who could land a customer much quicker than I ever could. I borrowed from the owner, fell into debt. I stopped going to Music and Art. The haberdasher's ate up more and more of my time. And I had no limousine service. I had to ride the local in and out of the Bronx. Each stop was a kind of purgatory. Freeman Street. Simpson Street. Intervale Avenue . . .

I did have a rescuer, and oddly enough it was the king of crime—not Costello himself, but one of his custodians. Count Dracula. He entered the shop with that whitewashed complexion of his, and all the clerks began to shiver. The haberdasher's couldn't have survived without his catalogues.

He halted in front of the shop's spindly owner. "I believe this young man owes you some gelt," he said, without ever pointing to me.

"It's nothing, Mr. R., honest to God. A trifle."

"A trifle?" Rosenzweig said, tossing him a wad of cash tied with a rubber band. "Shame on you, Paulie, taking advantage of such a fine young fellow. An artist, even. He's my own discovery. I met him at the Frick."

And then Rosenzweig came to my counter, his nostrils widening, as if he meant to suck all our men's furnishings into his nose like some magnificent anteater.

"Have you had your fill of selling cuff links? How long haven't you been to school?"

"Two weeks, Mr. Rosenzweig."

"A month," he said. "Did I ever keep you away from your books?"

He started to cry in front of the salesclerks. "Look what's become of you! You'll die here without the sunlight. We can't make do without our Adonis."

And the negotiations began. Count Dracula was all about negotiation, nothing else.

"I won't have dinner with war widows."

"All right," he said. "I'll say you're allergic to food. But you'll meet with them for fifteen minutes, right in the showroom."

"Ten," I said. "Not a minute more."

I collected all my things and went out the door with Dracula. We drove down to *Shmatahland* in his limousine. The streets were cluttered with men and boys wheeling enormous carts of merchandise—Seventh Avenue had a hum I've heard nowhere else, the sound of human traffic spinning off the walls of buildings, bouncing up and down, until the air itself was swollen with a soft, incessant noise that entered showrooms and factories right under the roofs. I wasn't sentimental about my stay in *Shmatahland*. I was a high-priced prisoner of war. But there was nothing diabolic about that noise. It was the hubbub of angels, brutal and busy, but angels nonetheless.

ARCHY AND MEHITABEL

I'd never heard of Archy and Mehitabel. The idea of a cockroach who could write poetry would have appealed to a kid from the Bronx. But I had to wait until I attended high school in Manhattan before I would learn about that cockroach and his companion, an alley cat who thought she was Cleopatra. The kids at Music and Art would quote line after line of Mehitabel's meditations while I nodded my head.

"Toujours gai, kid." That was her love cry to the cockroach.

I was smitten by Archy and Mehitabel, and by the swagger of all those M&Aers from Manhattan's Upper West Side. The boys wore white bucks, shoes that looked like anteaters or rumpled rats and were the favorite footwear among Ivy Leaguers. These boys had one ambition: to get into Harvard or Yale.

The girls weren't that different. They scribbled poems at night and practiced their acceptance speech for the Pulitzer Prize. I had a secret crush on one of them—Merle Messenger. It happened in the fall of '53. We were both sophomores in the same English class. She was tall and *zaftig*, with the ripeness of an opera star. She sang in the school choir and could have walked right into Julliard. But Merle didn't want a career in music. She wanted to teach world literature at one of the Seven Sisters. She read with a terrifying appetite. She had lavender eyes, like Elizabeth Taylor, and when she talked of Mehitabel or Natasha in *War and Peace*, those lavender eyes had all the little explosions of the Milky Way.

I was mute around Merle. The Bronx had very small purchase on West End Avenue. And I was startled when she asked me to study with her.

"You'll give me courage," she said. "I always shiver before an exam."

And so I visited Merle on a Friday night in November. It was like entering Ali Baba's den. The building had a doorman in a gray uniform, and elevator operators in identical gray. I had to announce myself. I was summoned into the lobby. One of the elevator men pulled on a golden lever and we shot upstairs in an ancient, shivering car.

Merle's mother met me at the door. She was president of the PTA at Music and Art. Her name was Yvonne. She wrote novels for young adults. Merle's father was a book critic for the *World-Telegram & Sun*.

He clapped his hands and Merle came out of her room. She was wearing slippers and gorgeous blue pajamas under a silk robe—that's how she dressed for a study date. Her mom and dad didn't even notice.

"Yvonne," said the book critic, "look what Merle has done. She's brought us Jerry Salinger's double. Doesn't he have Jerry's big ears?"

It's true. I did have big ears—and Salinger's brooding, dark demean.

"Ah," said Mrs. Messenger, "leave the kid alone. He's interested in your daughter, not J. D. Salinger."

Salinger reigned over the Upper West Side; half the kids at M&A knew his stuff by heart. But it took me an entire month to grasp that "Uncle Wiggily in Connecticut" and "The Laughing Man" were short stories rather than pickle merchants at the Jennings Street Market.

I walked hand in hand with Merle through an endless maze of dark rooms—West End Avenue had all the light of a sepulchre. And finally we came to her room, which was almost as large as our apartment in the Bronx. It had two beds, a sofa, and a desk near the window. Merle didn't believe in preludes or preambles. She undid her robe and let me glimpse at her partial nakedness in pajamas that almost served as a second skin.

She meant to play Manhattan's own alley cat and seduce a cockroach from the Bronx, but I was as much of a trickster as Merle. I moonlighted after class. I was a male model for a Seventh Avenue clothing cataloguer, Rosenzweig & Co. Girls were always running around the showroom in their panties and peekaboo bras. Romances would flare up behind a photographer's curtain. The whole place was a tinderbox.

It took me a while to understand the mechanics of Merle's household. Her mom and dad didn't like her running around to parties with college boys and coming home after midnight, smothered in mascara. They weren't snobs. I went to Music and Art and looked like J. D. Salinger. That was enough of a résumé.

I saw Merle once or twice a week, stayed over, and had breakfast with her mom and dad. But I was on a tightrope, since I had no time to read the books they talked about at the kitchen table—Kafka and his castle, Cervantes and his crackpot of a knight, James Joyce and the river that rattled through his bones.

Merle was the snob, not her mother. Whatever delight we took in the wonderful warp of our bodies didn't carry over to M&A. I wasn't included in that web of friends she had. She mocked me in our English class when I fumbled for the right word.

"What Jerome is trying to say, Dr. McCloud, is that Hamlet is dangerous to all mankind—he kills on the advice of a ghost. He'd marry his own mother if he had half the chance."

No one could argue with Merle. Literature was her own private tablet and proving ground. She could talk about a text as if she were in the middle of making love. Her sentences were a kind of intelligent delirium.

My hair began to fall out. Rosenzweig, the catalogue king, gave me a special shampoo. He sniffed the air with his huge nostrils, looking like Count Dracula with a whitewashed face. But he was gentle with me. I was his most successful protégé.

"I'm in love," I said.

Rosenzweig had a quick solution. I should overwhelm my sweetheart with *his* largesse. It sounded like a military operation. But I was desperate and listened to Dracula. I announced to Merle that we were going on a real date—beyond her bedroom. She wasn't very pleased, but she must have been curious. I showed up on West End Avenue in a maroon sport coat from Rosenzweig's racks. Merle was waiting for me in high heels and a miraculous silver gown. Her lavender eyes weakened whatever will I had. I was her Archy, the cockroach who couldn't type capital letters. And she was my myopic Mehitabel.

"Toujours gai, kid," she said as we approached the elevator. But she was suspicious of Rosenzweig's chauffeur and limousine.

"Am I your gun moll? And is this an armored car?"

She couldn't have realized how prescient she was. The limo and its driver had once belonged to Frank Costello, who was the cataloguer's silent partner.

Rosenzweig had picked the restaurant, a Florentine dive on Ninth Avenue that didn't have to troll for customers. Costello himself dined there whenever he wasn't in the clink. The waiters, who wore blue bow ties and tight little jackets, treated Merle like Cleopatra. They brought flowers to the table. They lit a long red candle. They served us wine, even though we were too young to drink in public. They wouldn't let us order from the menu.

"Darlings, you'll eat what Mr. Frank eats."

We had a Tuscan appetizer—crushed tomatoes and olives

on flat bread. We had a salad of tiny green and yellow stalks. We had linguine cooked in the chef's own white wine sauce. We had chicken breasts baked with onions, walnuts, and diced ham . . .

Merle may have been myopic, but she wasn't blind. The restaurant was a haven for top-tier gangsters and their Madonnas, or mistress-wives. Some of these Madonnas were even younger than Merle. She never asked me who "Mr. Frank" was. But her lavender eyes were like needles after her second sip of wine. I was heartsick. There wasn't any way to win. I couldn't woo her with literature. I'd taken her out of her own little cave and had revealed nothing but a garish world of gunmen.

We rode back to West End Avenue in utter silence. She wouldn't even let me hold her hand. And she didn't invite me upstairs. I'd disappointed her more than I could ever have imagined. And she was quite cruel.

"Jerome, I think you'd better stick to your armored car. If you cruise long enough, you might find some poor Ophelia . . . and maybe the two of you can run off together and drown. Goodnight, my sweet, sweet prince."

There were no more study dates. Merle never glanced at me once in the halls of Music and Art. Her lavender eyes went right through my skin and bones. Still, I was probably the richest kid at M&A. Rosenzweig cheated me, but he couldn't afford to cheat me too much. The catalogues were his bread and butter, and I was his most popular item.

But I felt cheated out of my childhood. I slaved like a dog after school. I wore white bucks, but the time I spent in the showroom kept me from my studies and pulled me far, far from New Haven and Harvard Yard.

I heard through the grapevine at M&A that Merle Messenger had fallen in love with a Harvard frosh. She arrived at school in a crimson sweatshirt, wearing a Harvard pin. She'd snub her friends, stare at the ceiling, yawn while Dr. McCloud talked of Thomas Hardy and *Jude the Obscure*, and then she didn't come to school at all.

The West Siders swore she had eloped with that crimson boy and was living in a cabin on Mount Rainier. I didn't believe a word of it, but I couldn't borrow Rosenzweig's limo and ride to Seattle. And the farther away I was from Merle, the more I missed our nights together and my breakfasts with the Messengers.

And then, six months after Merle had disappeared, I saw Mrs. Messenger at Music and Art. That should have been enough of a hint that Merle wasn't on Mount Rainier.

"Mr. Salinger," she said with a teasing smile, "Merle would like to see you."

I started to shiver in my pants. "I don't get it. Hasn't she gone away?"

"She never left Manhattan. She's been hospitalized, but now she's back home. She was suicidal—for a couple of weeks."

At first I thought the crimson boy had broken her heart, but there was no crimson boy, according to Mrs. M. It was all part of Merle's "liquid imagination."

I didn't know what to bring—candy or flowers? But I brought nothing at all. I didn't want Merle to feel I was visiting a mental patient.

Her face was as white as Count Dracula's. All her fleshiness had disappeared in six months. But her lavender eyes still bled with the fierceness of the Milky Way. She had gates on her windows now. And the shadows of the buildings across the street overwhelmed her room. We could have been in some netherworld.

"How is tricks?" I asked in Archy's vernacular.

She began to purr like an alley cat. "Still a lady," she said. "There's a dance or two in the old dame yet." Then the purring stopped, and I could see the taut lines under Mehitabel's mask. "You should have socked me. That might have pulled me out of my delirium."

"But you weren't delirious."

"Yes, I was. That's why Daddy never liked me to go out on dates."

"But you functioned beautifully at school. You'll be our valedictorian."

"School," she said, frowning a bit. "That's like brushing my teeth in the dark. It's a part I've been playing since kindergarten. All Mommy had to do was wind me up—darling, haven't you ever noticed the key carved into my back?"

There was no key, and there never had been. But I wouldn't contradict her.

"Merle, your father should have told me, and I wouldn't have taken you to that awful restaurant."

"But Daddy adores you. And I adored the funny little men who served us."

"You didn't have such a hot time," I said.

"But it wasn't the restaurant—it was the light."

I didn't understand. That Florentine dive was like a dungeon, because Mr. Frank and his lieutenants preferred not to be seen around strangers.

"The candles," she said. "It hurt my eyes to watch them flicker on the wall. I was irritable. I took it out on you. I turn into a witch whenever I'm away from this room."

"Then it's a good geography lesson. We'll limit ourselves to this terrain."

She frowned again. "There are no limits, dear Jerome. Haven't you heard of William Blake? You can hold Infinity in the palm of your hand."

And I had my Infinity in a dark room on West End Avenue with gates on the windows. There were no sentinels outside Merle's door. Her mom and dad never spied on us. I spent as many nights with Merle as I could. Dracula's driver delivered me from the showroom to West End Avenue. I'd become the paterfamilias of my own little tribe in the East Bronx. Rosenzweig's accountant handled all my bills. And I explained to my mom and dad that it was much more efficient for me to reside in Manhattan overnight.

I borrowed Merle's liquid imagination and recast the Messengers into my own parents. It was a dangerous high-wire act. Young J. D. Salinger in their daughter's bed. But they weren't shopping for a son-in-law, just a guy who kept Merle out of harm's way.

I loved her, even with her face as white as chalk. I cherished every scrap of flesh on her bones. She was hungry all the time. Merle ate two meals for every meal I ate, and she was *zaftig* again after a month.

It was only then that she confided in me and confessed what the hell had happened. She hadn't tried to kill herself, not really. She'd just scribbled on the bathroom wall with her own blood.

TOUJOURS GAI, KID

Mommy and Daddy sent her to the sanatorium. And there had been a crimson boy, but he wasn't from Harvard. He was an orderly, fond of wearing a red hospital coat. His name was Marvin, and he was from Brighton Beach. He read poetry to Merle while she was strapped to a bed. Marvin knocked her up. She had an abortion and was shipped home to West End Avenue.

"I wanted to marry him," she said. "Marvin made love to me, right after he fed me lunch. Daddy had him sent to some kind of Siberia for disgraced orderlies."

I was broken with jealousy. I envied that crimson boy and the time he had with Merle in the madhouse.

"Marvin still writes. But Mommy tears up all his letters."

And then she would take me inside her blue pajamas as if we were comrades in arms, and I had my own small portion of Infinity with Merle. I was like some pale replica of that crimson boy.

She talked of going back to M&A.

Some mountebank of a doctor was called in. He examined Merle for two hours.

"Jerome," Merle whispered after the mountebank left. "We'll study together."

But I knew what would happen next. Her lavender eyes seduced everyone in sight. She didn't even have to make up the term she had missed. She sang in the school choir. We were in Dr. McCloud's creative writing class. Her stories and poems were chiseled dreams from her days and nights in a madhouse. None of us could compete with Merle. And I couldn't write about Rosenzweig & Co., or I would have been chucked out of school.

Merle was back with her old clique. They smoked in the toilet, talked about Radcliffe and the rest of the Seven Sisters. And soon she was much too occupied with choir practice to have study dates.

I realized I was out on my ass after Mrs. M.'s maid returned the underwear she had ironed to my Bronx address. I worked more hours at the showroom. Other cataloguers tried to lure me away.

"Over my dead body," Rosenzweig said, sniffling into a handkerchief. But it was a big act. Who would have been insane enough to mess with Mr. Frank's silent partner? Dracula tossed a wad of hundred-dollar bills at me.

"Ingrate," he said. "Eat my heart out."

I stopped wearing white bucks. I fell away from that elite gang of West Siders. Yale was just another school in some wilderness of towers. I thought of dropping out of M&A.

Rosenzweig began to pull out my hair. And I was precious to him. He might have ruined his own product.

"I don't have dropouts in my stable. Stupidity is not an option for one of my models."

"Big talker," I said. "What if I should get into Harvard by some stroke of luck?"

His nostrils were flaring again. "I'll feel as proud as if it was my own son."

"Ah, but it's not so simple to commute from Seventh Avenue to Cambridge, Mass."

And he mocked his protégé "With my drivers, kid, it's a piece of cake."

I didn't have a real home—not the garment district, not the Bronx, and not West End Avenue. My grades suffered. I avoided Merle and her whole clique. If we happened to pass in the corridors, her eyes would scrape the ceiling and mine would scrape the walls.

I was going to skip graduation, but I didn't want to disappoint my mom and dad. They arrived on Convent Avenue in one of Dracula's limousines, Mom clutching a cane. I couldn't sit with them; I was up front with all the graduates, in my gown. We had a guest speaker, some Manhattan potentate, but I didn't listen to his blather. I was waiting for the valedictorian. She strode to the platform like the Valkyrie she had become in her senior year. She'd been accepted at all Seven Sisters and chose Barnard, because she wouldn't have to give up her lair on West End Avenue.

And she spoke to us with all the aplomb of her new sisterhood. She sang about the goodwill of graduating seniors—our desire to serve. She even mentioned bomb shelters and the Cold War. But I could feel her body breathe under the maroon graduation gown with a wildness of its own.

Merle winked at us and said, "Now I'd like to talk about Archy, a cockroach who was punished for having been a poet in his former life. Poetry matters to him. And it matters to his companion, Mehitabel, who would rather be 'rowdy and gaunt . . . than slaves to a tame society.'"

Merle stared down from the lectern, into the dimmed lights. "That is our credo at M&A. We prefer dissonance and cacophony to familiar sounds."

Merle's classmates whistled and tossed their graduation caps into the air—that is, all her classmates except one. I couldn't gamble as much as Merle did. I was already an entrepreneur, under Rosenzweig's wing. But I disappointed Dracula. I hadn't applied to Harvard or Yale—I needed a sabbatical year between high school and college. I had to break my addiction to the Ivy League.

I tried to sneak out of the ceremonies, but Merle's own mom blocked my way. She was sniffling into a handkerchief. "Wasn't that a gorgeous speech, Jerome?"

She must have noticed the darkness under my eyes.

Suddenly her shoulders were trembling.

"It's my fault. I encouraged Merle to bring you home. You weren't part of her usual crowd. There wouldn't be any complication with parents."

"Yeah," I said. "It was a lark. I could sleep over, comfort Merle."

"It was better than having her run around with strangers."

"And I was her trusted rag doll. I was crazy about your daughter. I would have learned to disappear with much more gusto and grace. But you should have told me about that crimson boy."

Her eyes bulged. She looked like a bird of prey. "What crimson boy?"

"The orderly who knocked up Merle."

"Young man," she said, "I'll have your diploma rescinded if you breathe another word. My daughter loves to lie."

And Mrs. Messenger vanished into that maroon world of graduation gowns.

I didn't ride home with my parents in the limousine. I strolled through West Harlem in my cap and gown. I followed Broadway down to the garment district. Men on milk boxes saluted me. A housewife with wondrous hips flirted with the young graduate. I danced with her for a second in the street. She licked my ear. All I could think of was Merle in her blue pajamas.

THE CAT LADY'S KISS

She'd never been kissed by a man, never even fumbled around on the dunes of Orchard Beach. She lost her cherry to Queen Donadio, the head cashier at the Italian market on Arthur Avenue. It wasn't love, or anything like that. Angela must have been fifteen, and the cashier kept eyeballing her one afternoon until she felt hypnotized, so she followed Queenie into the storage room. Angela didn't have to do a thing. Queenie plucked off Angela's clothes, and without a word of warning began to nibble between her legs. Most of Queenie's scalp had vanished, and Angela didn't know whether to laugh or cry. It was like having a wet tickle. And then she started to moan in rhythm to the maniacal wanderings of Queenie's tongue, and she let out a cry that was like the mooing of a cow robbed of all her milk.

Queenie dropped her after that, didn't even say one word of hello, and it wouldn't have mattered, because Angela got into trouble. Her mother was away in a mental hospital, and her father never worked; he kept sniffing around whenever Angela had her period. She didn't have the heart to punish her own *papi*. They were starving, and Angela began to steal—at first it was bread and apples to keep them alive, and then she became a bandit in the Bronx, stealing purses from old ladies. One of the old ladies yelled too loud, and Angela beat her over the head to stop all the yelling. The woman started to cackle and had a stroke.

Angela sat in a juvenile facility, and was sent off in shackles to a prison farm the minute she turned seventeen. She had to punk for the trustees and older inmates, who looked after her and saw to Angela's education. She even finished high school at the farm. Part of her education was a floating film club: an unfrocked professor would wander from prison farm to prison farm with a DVD player and a whole bag of films out of the 1940s. The one Angela liked best was about a woman who turned into a ferocious cat whenever a man tried to kiss her; even her husband couldn't kiss this cat lady, who might have torn him to ribbons, fond of him as she was.

The older inmates would laugh and say, "Yeah, she would have loved him to death." And they began to call Angela the cat lady who'd never been kissed by a man.

She was twenty-one when she left the farm. She returned to the Bronx with an institutional gray complexion. She went to work at the market on Arthur Avenue. The new head cashier was a man named Robertson. He was a jailbird, like Angela, with his own gray pall. He must have been forty. He had big ears and hands as soft and smooth as a girl's. He wouldn't leave off looking at Angela.

Robertson was quite clever with his hands. He would construct figures out of stray pieces of wire, twist that wire into walruses and lithe, prowling cats. And when he gave these wire figures to Angela, his fingers trembled. He never leered at her once or touched her behind. He was like a strange, balding knight with big ears.

Angela didn't know what to do about Robertson. She felt a slight tug in her loins, but it frightened her. "Miss Angela," he said, after six months of silent, stubborn courtship. "I sure as hell would like it if we could make love."

"Where?" she asked, already imagining him ripped to shreds.

"Where else? In the storage room."

"Mr. Robertson, it would have to be at your own risk."

But her balding knight walked her into the storage room and bolted the door from inside. He touched her face. She began to purr, but it quickly became a growl.

"Mr. Robertson, do what you want with me. But we can't kiss. I'm the cat lady. And loving me might mean your own death."

He undressed her with his beautiful soft hands.

"I wish," he said, "I wish I could shape you out of wire."

"Mr. Robertson, you already did. I'm that prowling wire cat."

He stroked her flanks, ran his fingers across her breasts until her nipples were taut and fierce as knives.

"Mr. Robertson, you'll have to make me wet. I've never been with a man."

He wouldn't stoop between her legs. He kept stroking Angela with his soft hands until her whole body quaked. But the more he aroused her, the more she felt her whiskers grow. He hovered near her mouth. Her thighs tingled, tingled with dread.

She thought of her father, who had tried to rape her with his wrinkled prick. Perhaps she was the cat lady long before she'd gone to the prison farm, waiting for her father to kiss her, so she could rip out his throat and claw him blind. Poor Papi, she sang to herself, as her own storage-room magician kept fondling her with his soft hands.

And now she knew why this balding knight appealed to her. He had Papi's big ears and famished look. Her mother had been out of her mind ever since Angela was a child, trying to stick her own head into the oven, hovering on the fire escape in her nightgown, and being led off to the asylum.

"Angela," she had wept, "your father stopped fucking me five minutes after you were born. You're his new bride."

And little Angela would walk to kindergarten pretending to

wear a bride's veil. But it made no sense being married to Papi, who snored all the time and smelled like a goat. And she tore her own pretended veil.

And now she was in the same storage room where Queenie had licked her to the edge of madness seven years ago. But she didn't miss Queenie. She had Robertson, the jailbird, who began to hum under his breath, and her body stirred to that whispering music. He was shaping her with his hands, turning her into a wire creature.

She growled once, but it was no less a song than Robertson's.

His lips grazed hers. Her mouth opened into a sweet well. His tongue tasted of cinnamon cloves and cherries on a tree. She ripped at him, but her paws didn't leave a mark. His tongue went deep. Robertson had learned how to survive a cat lady's kiss.

He grew morose within a week. And Angela wondered if he was as fickle as Queenie. But it wasn't that. A hopeless gambler, he had lost a bundle to the Albanians, who had come to Arthur Avenue with their own "caravans"—rag shops and rinky-dink cafés and social clubs, which the Italians tolerated because these donkeys from Albania kept Latinos from overwhelming Arthur Avenue and turning it into a second South Bronx.

The Albanians never bought property. They rented from Italian landlords and didn't interfere with the local mob bosses. These donkeys had become the enforcers of the Neapolitan social club, which had dominion over Arthur Avenue and the Belmont section of the Bronx. But Belmont was a landlocked island surrounded by the Latino wild men of Tremont and Fordham Road. It was the natural barriers of the Bronx Zoo and Quarry Road that kept the wild men away from Belmont—Arthur Avenue was hard to find—and also the Albanians, who had their own wild men. Their chieftain was Lord Lekë, and he held sway over Bathgate Avenue, at the ragged edge of the old Italian neighborhood.

It was this Albanian wild man who coveted Angela, had seen her in the market, had thought of kidnapping her, but didn't want to bring an earthquake to Arthur Avenue. So he sent out his spies on a reconnaissance mission. They discovered her with that jailbird, Robertson, who was a complete outsider, having grown up in Montana or some other place that didn't really exist in the minds of the Albanians. Lord Lekë and his clan sucked him deeper and deeper into their gambling dens, offered him access to their own harem of whores, and then put the screws on him. Either Robertson signed Angela over to his clan or Lekë would send him to live with the snow leopards in the Bronx Zoo.

"But Miss Angela is not a cow," the jailbird tried to reason. "And I cannot sign her over to you, Lord Lekë."

"But you could persuade her about my charms. . . . She doesn't have to live on Bathgate Avenue. All she has to do is visit me once, and I will cancel your debt."

Despite his fears, Robertson couldn't present such a proposal to Angela. All he could do was twist his pieces of wire into some miniature of Lekë's long nose and winter cape. And Angela, who'd been through the medieval rites and rituals of prison life, understood right away.

"That Albanian bastard thinks your markers are also mine, and that he can paw me whenever he wants."

Robertson didn't say a word. His eyes practically disappeared inside his skull, and Angela knew that he would either fall into his own mad oblivion or run away. But he didn't run. And one morning he failed to show up at work. Angela found him across Quarry Road, at St. Barnabas. His face was a mask of bruises. And Angela couldn't see much else under his hospital gown.

She started to cry. "Why didn't you run home to Montana?"

"My home is in the Bronx," he said, "with you."

He'd continued his wire menagerie on the night table near his bed. Leopards and rhinos, ostriches and giraffes, like the inhabitants of some new Noah's ark. She visited him every evening after work, sat beside him, and after having sworn to herself that she'd never knit, sew, or cook for a man, she knit her balding knight a sweater. But St. Barnabas couldn't hold him forever.

So Angela did what she had to do. She couldn't have gone to the Neapolitans at their club, because she was a Latina and a little freak who liked women as much as men. She'd never been to Bathgate Avenue before, though it was five minutes from the market where she worked. She'd seen the Albanians at Dominick's; they always occupied the last two tables, always ate alone; they brought their own cotton napkins, their own knives and forks, and if one of the Neapolitan lords entered the restaurant, they would salute him with their wine glasses and return to their incredible gluttony. Dominick's had no menus, only markers on the wall. But each Albanian went through Dominick's secret repertoire of pasta dishes, each had a salad meant for five, and five espressos served in little glasses. They were never boisterous, and they never asked for the bill. They would bow to the waiter and hand him an envelope stuffed with cash.

Angela knew the Albanians were taking their own time. They would swallow up Arthur Avenue in ten or twenty years, imprison the Neapolitans inside their own club without ever declaring a state of war. She recognized how shrewd their chieftain was, Lekë with his long nose, his brutal blond looks, his thick hands, and the winter cape he wore no matter what the season. He'd seen Angela across the dining room with its row after row of communal tables, had sent her a flower and a glass of coffee, which she realized must have been some kind of Albanian ritual. But she wouldn't respond. She never did, no matter how many times the coffees came in their little glasses. And now she had to prevent her bald knight from being beaten to death.

The Albanians of Bathgate Avenue had no church. They were agnostics who might have preserved a few Muslim, Christian, and Jewish signs. Albanian farmers and bandits had protected the Jews during the German occupation of their country. Not one Jew was delivered to the Gestapo or the SS. Some of the bandits began wearing skullcaps as a mark of respect; they never violated Jewish women. Stars of David and Jewish candelabra remained in Albanian homes long after the war.

And that's what Angela found in the windows of Bathgate Avenue; Jewish stars and candelabra mingled with crosses and paintings of Jesus. She didn't waver for a minute. She walked into Lekë's social club, even though the door had been painted black and there was a sign that said CATS AND STRANGERS NOT ALLOWED. She'd entered a cavern where money flew like feathers; she'd never seen such an enterprise. Men wagered over bundles of sticks, threw chess pieces into the air like lucky coins, and mutilated deck after deck as they tore up cards they didn't happen to like. There were women at the tables wearing head scarves; they gambled with the men. They were obedient and insolent in the same breath, bowing to Lekë and his lieutenants, who sat on enormous pillows, and taunting them with their eyes.

They seemed frightened of Angela, who wore no scarf and did not bow to any of the gamblers. Lekë stared at her from his pasha's pillow—a blue-eyed Albanian. Angela navigated among the horde of gamblers, propelled by her love for that balding knight at St. Barnabas, and paused near the pasha's cowboy boots. The social club was silent as a mouse.

"Lord Lekë, we have things to discuss."

He laughed. "Have you come to seek employment, my little cashier?"

The Albanians chortled and clapped their hands. "Lord," one of his lieutenants shouted, "put her to work on her back."

And the women laughed louder than the men, causing their head scarves to ripple.

"Quiet," Lekë said. "Show the lady some respect. . . . I have no secrets from my men, Miss Angela. We are a family—Michael, make her some tea!"

Lekë's minions served Angela tea in a glass that was much too hot to hold, but she held it anyhow, drank the bittersweet water. They served her little cakes—almond tarts with raspberry cream at the bottom. But no one asked her to sit, and all of a sudden she was the only one in this dark den who was still standing. It was a cave in the middle of the Bronx, with images of some medieval prince on the wall. He had a handlebar mustache, bushy eyebrows, and long curly hair; he wore a kind of skullcap, an embroidered jacket, and sticking out of his cummerbund was a knife encrusted with jewels. He was, she would learn, Lekë Dukagjini, a fifteenth-century mountain prince who fought against the Turks and instituted his own highland code, which governed tribal warfare; in this code women could govern as well as men, and there were many "virgin warriors" among the Dukagjinis, women who fought and dressed as mountain men. A popular myth was that all Albanians were descended from this one warrior-prince, who watered the highland lakes and many a mountain woman with his sperm and his blood; he lost his limbs in battle, dispatched ten thousand Turks. And the current prince of Bathgate Avenue was named after this ferocious man, as one of his lieutenants explained while she sipped her tea.

Lord Lekë was responsible for the welfare of every single Albanian in the Bronx. Daughters could not be married without his consent. Old men would come to him at any hour in fits of depression. Their lord would heal them with a bear hug and a hot glass of tea. He would appear at births and deaths, but he himself had fathered no one, did not have a child. And that is why his minions were so curious about the woman next to his cowboy boots. Was their *baba* in love?

She bowed to him. "You must not harm my fiancé. How has he wronged you?"

"He exists," said Lord Lekë. "That is enough of a wound. He blocks my avenue, mamzelle."

"And what avenue could that be?" Angela asked like a counselor-at-law.

"My avenue from me to you."

But she outsmarted this Bronx mountain bandit. She meant to murder him in front of all his minions—with a cat lady's kiss.

"You are mistaken, my lord. He hasn't blocked this avenue at all. Haven't I come to your club?"

"To plead for his life."

"Not at all," she said, and she could feel her whiskers growing. "Would my lord care for a kiss?"

But she didn't understand Bronx mountain lore. No woman, descended from the Dukagjinis or not, could demand a kiss from Lord Lekë, the *baba* of the Bronx. It was Lekë's right to appear in a woman's bedroom and ravish her, even with a husband at her side—it brought luck and long life to copulate with their lord, and husbands often delivered their own wives to Lord Lekë, but he wouldn't ravish them. He kissed them on the forehead and sent them home.

The lord's minions surrounded Angela with a menacing air. Lekë rose off his pillow to rant at them.

"Brothers, you will insult your king if you hurt this lady. She is a Latina. She does not understand our ways. . . . You must escort her home."

He collapsed onto his pillow and closed his eyes. Meanwhile, a horde of men and women accompanied her to Arthur Avenue like some miraculous honor guard.

She couldn't even find her balding knight. He vanished from St. Barnabas, left a note and a thousand dollars in crisp new bills.

> Angela, I have a very small future here.
> Your loving friend, Robertson

She wouldn't return to that madcap social club with all its riddles. She waited until Lord Lekë appeared at Dominick's with his clan. And while he sampled the pasta dishes with a look of utter ravishment, she went up to him and tossed the thousand dollars into his eyes. The rapture was gone, but he would allow none of his minions to rise from the table.

"What is my crime, Miss Angela?"

"You sent my man away and had him throw silver into my eyes—a thousand dollars."

"I did no such thing," said this lord of the Albanians. "I invited your fiancé to leave. I paid him, yes, but it wasn't blood money or a bribe. And it was much, much more than a thousand. He swindled you, I think. Mine was an honest proposal. I could break his leg or he could have a monthly stipend from me. He took the stipend. Sit down. Join us at the table, and my men will worship you forever. You'll be our queen."

Angela was trembling now. "Keep away from me, or I'll rip your heart out."

Lord Lekë began to laugh. "Children, she has fire. . . . Don't bring me heiresses, or lady bankers. My heart is locked. I will have no one but her as my bride, or I'll never marry."

She had never seen such imbecilic stubbornness, except in her father. She considered moving away from Arthur Avenue, abandoning the Bronx. This lord wouldn't have much sway outside the borough. Manhattan wasn't so fond of Albanians, who couldn't seem to flourish without the hills and highlands of the Bronx. But why should she run away? She'd lived here all her life, except for her own hard time in the prison farm. Her mother had been the janitor at an apartment house on Crescent Avenue before she went mad. The landlord had given them a ground-floor apartment in that building. The neighborhood had adopted little Angela. She'd worked behind the provolone stand at the Arthur Avenue indoor market when she was twelve, loved to watch the cigar makers, the widows with their little stash of stationery or their pots and pans. She remembered the chicken slaughterer who used to be at the end of the block, with feathers and squirts of blood in the window. Her *papi* would earn a few dollars wringing the chickens' necks. And he could never rid himself of the chicken scales on his hands, or that horrendous smell of death.

He still had that smell, years after the chicken slaughterer vanished from Arthur Avenue. He sat in their small apartment like a man whose own madness had set him on fire but who didn't have enough substance to really burn—one day he would shrivel up and shrink into the atmosphere, shoes and all. But when she returned home after her trip to Bathgate Avenue, Papi wasn't there. Neither was the furniture, nor Angela's narrow bed. The apartment could have been swept clean by locusts.

Had the landlord reclaimed the apartment after all these years? But where the hell was Papi? And then the landlord appeared with a nervous grin. He couldn't even look into Angela's eyes. He'd rented the apartment to a plumber and moved Angela upstairs to the fifth floor. He wouldn't even raise her rent.

So she climbed to the fifth floor, and there was Papi sitting like a potentate. The new apartment looked out onto the red behemoth of St. Barnabas and the jagged landscape of the Bronx, cut in half by an expressway, which had turned everything around it into a vast moonscape of flattened warehouses and empty lots. She had been born after the expressway was built, and that's why she clung to the little oasis of Arthur Avenue, which was just beyond that moonscape and did not preside over its ruin.

But Angela wasn't a Bronx moocow. She was clever enough to know who the landlord's "plumber" was—Lord Lekë. He hadn't bought the apartment house, which belonged to the little kingdom of Arthur Avenue. He'd finessed the Italian chieftains by renting Angela's apartment at a million times what it was worth, she imagined, and thus allowing the landlord to "lend" his prize apartment near the roof to a scruffy old man with his dyke of a daughter.

She couldn't ask the landlord to give her back the apartment on the ground floor. She'd never even had a lease. Angela was caught in some kind of crazy wind. It was like the chess pieces the Albanians tossed into the air. No one knew where the pawns and knights would land.

The wild man left begonias outside her door—begonias, bracelets, and diamond rings. She couldn't accept such gifts. It would have meant that she belonged to Lekë, even if he hadn't come to claim her. She didn't have the slightest desire to return to Little Albania. So she scribbled a note to Lord Lekë and left it on his table at Dominick's.

> My Lord, you must take back your presents.
> I am not in love with you and never will be.

It didn't take long for the wild man to respond. Several of the clan's wives appeared in head scarves, took Angela by the hand, and accompanied her to Lekë's stronghold, which wasn't even in Little Albania but was on the Grand Concourse, near Fordham Road, in Latino territory. The cops held no sway here. The neighborhood was called Paradise Road, in honor of a nearby movie palace that had once been the crown jewel of the West Bronx, with an "atmospheric" indoor sky, filled with stars and wandering clouds. Angela was born a little too late, after the Loew's Paradise had been chopped into pieces, its ornate statues and staircases removed, and its immortal sky went dark, while Paradise Road itself was embroiled in a drug war. But the Albanians had pushed the drug lords aside, and even if Paradise Road wasn't part of Lekë's kingdom, the Latino warlords left him alone.

He occupied the penthouse of an Art Deco palace that local architects and builders had put up eighty years ago, when the Grand Concourse was the Bronx's own Jewish boulevard. A Concourse millionaire had lived in the penthouse. Lekë moved in after the millionaire fled to Palm Beach and the Concourse grew into a wild land. Paradise Road had sharpshooters reigning from the roofs. The drug lords had put them there. But after a while the sharpshooters were bored to death and would pick off children and old men . . . until Lekë had them hurled off the roofs.

The building had an Albanian doorman, who signaled with his cell that Angela had arrived and rode upstairs with her in an elevator that had a silver ceiling. She was startled by the penthouse. It didn't have one image of Lekë's ancestors on the walls, no Dukagjini in fierce tribal dress, with battle-axes and rivers of blood. Lekë himself didn't seem so fierce away from his clan. He greeted Angela in a silken robe.

"Lord, you must not send me diamond rings."

"And why not?" he asked in a softer voice, without so much gravel. "You're the one I intend to marry."

"I'll never marry you, sire, even if you have my father thrown into the street."

"Ah," he said, "now I'll have that kiss you promised me in our gambling hall."

Her whiskers were sprouting again, but she felt sorry for this warrior-king who kept sending her diamonds, and she was in no mood to maul him.

"Sire, my kisses could be fatal."

He pulled her close to him. She could smell the wild man's perfume. Angela herself began to feel strange and confused, even a little dizzy. She could hear Lekë's heart beat under his silk robe. She started to growl. The wild man rubbed against her. Her tongue darted into his mouth. His robe loosened. The lord of all the Albanians in the Bronx had a clit.

They were married within a month, not at a chapel, but in the cave on Bathgate Avenue. Angela's *papi* was there; so were members of the Neapolitan social club and the Latino lord of Paradise Road. Angela was dressed in white. She'd invited a few of her sisters from the farm, who had come to the wedding on a weekend pass. These sisters were startled to see *their* cat lady as a bride. How could they have known that this blond assassin and warlord was sometimes a lady and sometimes a man? He'd been wearing men's clothes ever since he was five. Lekë had come to America at fifteen, took over Little Albania before he was twenty. None of his subjects suspected that he wasn't always a man, though Albania had a long history of hunters and kings who went into battle smeared with their own menstrual blood.

Lekë was often filled with gloom. That's why he gravitated to the Grand Concourse. He could sport around as a woman or a man in his penthouse along Paradise Road. And he could also sport with his bride. He'd been in love with Angela from the moment he saw her in the Italian market, with that sad, beautiful face and the lithe body of a jailbird, and he would have destroyed a whole army of Robertsons to have her.

She couldn't always tell whether she was making love to a woman or a man—Lord Lekë was both. He wasn't like Angela's muscle-bound sisters at the farm, whose lust was limited to conquering all the new "chickens." Lekë was always gentle with her, and it was the gentleness of a man. Angela was now queen of all the Dukagjinis, who doted on her and waited for a male heir.

She'd never been happy, not once in her life, until the king claimed her as his bride. But it was Lekë who seemed forlorn.

"I'd like to throw it over," he said. "This pathetic charade of kingliness . . . all my little lords, with their male jokes. I'd love to crush their skulls. I promise you, I'll go to my next meet wearing a dress."

"Lekë darling, you've never worn a dress in your life."

He came down off his hill one afternoon and was seen wearing lipstick and a scowl while he sat with his lieutenants. What could he have said to these young, ambitious hunters of his clan? Did he have to remind them that the Dukagjinis had had other women warriors? Did they all laugh and toss little wooden knights into the air?

He survived until the next afternoon. While Angela was out walking with a bodyguard, his own hunters threw him off the terrace. They buried him at Woodlawn, traveling in a long procession to their own family plot, but without Angela, who was no longer recognized as their queen. They removed all her clothes from the penthouse. She returned to Papi's fifth-floor apartment on Crescent Avenue. He didn't even say a word, just looked at her with his bloodshot eyes, and howled once. It could have been the sound of her own heart. Her cash ran out after a month and she had to go back to work at the Italian market. It was almost as if she'd never been gone, as if she'd dreamt of that warrior-king from Little Albania, so near to Arthur Avenue and so far away.

SILK & SILK

Marla Silk grew up amid that solid wall of Art Deco palaces along Central Park West. Her father was involved in some mystery called arbitrage. Marla loved to tell her friends at Fieldston that his name, Mortimer Silk, was only a mask—the Silks were Marranos who had had to change their identity hundreds of years ago as they moved from Spain to Morocco.

Daddy had made quite a stir on Wall Street when he bet against the dollar and sank all the money of Silk & Silk into deutschmarks. For one or two days he must have owned half the deutschmarks in the world; and then Daddy dumped the whole lot. Marla was notorious after that at her own high school.

She had the SATs of a rocket scientist. Marla picked Columbia, because she couldn't leave her mom all alone. Mother was like a sleepwalker at Saks, and she got high on ice cream sodas every afternoon at Rumpelmayer's. Marla would join her when she could, while Mother wept in a mad fever. Her name was Lollie. She'd been Mortimer's campus sweetheart at Ohio State. Lollie was a Lutheran from Kansas.

"Your mother was willowy." That's how Mortimer had described her. "No one could keep his eyes off her for very long. She had the longest legs in the world. Lollie was born too late.

She should have been with the Ziegfeld Follies. Manhattan overwhelms her. That's what she says."

Marla did her own bit of penance and sat on one of the stools at Rumpelmayer's. She'd rather have suffered through a whiskey sour, but Marla was only seventeen at the time, surrounded by nurses and nannies with their aristocratic charges and by dowagers who never missed a lunch at Rumpelmayer's. Lollie painted her face white while she was in that pink world, with teddy bears in the window. Mother was still in her thirties, and it was as if she had been fossilized and remained the campus queen—with a white, white face. She shouldn't have married Daddy, a brooder from the Bronx. He'd grown up along the Grand Concourse, among a hoard of Marrano merchants. Had Mother married some king of extracurricular activities at Ohio State, she might have been better off.

And now she was locked into endless lunches and teas at Rumpelmayer's. The waiters knew her, and so did the manager and the concierge at the St. Moritz. She was their local celebrity—Mortimer Silk's wife. But Marla couldn't bear to see Lollie sit in her white mask.

"Mummy," Marla would say, dizzy from the aroma of Rumpelmayer's dark chocolate. "You can't sit here forever."

"Why not? I might meet a nice man—a guest at the St. Moritz. An uncomplicated cattle rancher, or someone like that."

Rumpelmayer's did belong to the St. Moritz, so Mother's mind was intact, even if there was a bit of folly in what she said.

"Mother, you already have a man. And what would a cattle rancher be doing at the St. Moritz?"

"Looking for what's precious . . . like the grazing rights to Central Park. Now scram! I don't need to be plagued by my own daughter."

"Yes, you do," Marla said. But she couldn't have a battle royal with her own mother at Rumpelmayer's. She had to let her list all her grievances against Daddy and wait for that brush fire to burn out. And then they'd walk home together along the park.

Marla graduated summa cum laude and went on to Columbia Law. And after passing her bar exams, she became an in-house lawyer at Silk & Silk. She had no ambition to work anywhere else. "Silks have to serve Silks" was Mortimer's motto. Meanwhile, Marla had married her high school beau, Raphael, who also went to work for the Silks. She had two lovely daughters with Rafe—Candice and Lollie Jr.

Marla realized that Lollie Jr. wasn't a proper name for a girl. Lollie Jr. loved her name. She was as willful and enterprising as Marla, and talked about building empires by the time she was ten.

But Lollie Sr. grew worse and worse. Marla no longer had the time to rescue her from Rumpelmayer's. She and Rafe lived in the very same palace as Daddy, but on a lesser floor. Mother had to have a full-time nurse. She sank into a profound melancholy, and neither Marla nor Lollie Jr. could bring her out. Still, her own decline wasn't as steep as Mortimer's.

Suddenly there were auditors and bloodhounds all over the place, and Silk & Silk was padlocked for a week. Daddy was indicted. You could watch him on the evening news as he was whisked out of his apartment-palace in handcuffs. He could have been an axe murderer in a velvet coat. That's how crazed he looked. The witch right behind him was Marla, who didn't even have a minute to comb her hair. Daddy was arraigned and released on bail. He returned to his castle like some woebegone man. "I'll kill myself," he told Marla. The government had stool pigeons inside Silk & Silk and witnesses against Mortimer at rival arbitrage houses.

He'd swindled when he had to swindle, had walked a very thin line between what was legal and what was not. And now Daddy faced twenty years at some government facility in Kansas. He would have to sit and groan with other white-collar criminals. His handsome mane was on the cover of the *Post*. He was called "Silk, the Confidence Man."

Daddy sulked and sat with egg stains on his satin robe. He was fifty-seven and his face was whiter than Lollie's had ever been. One of his hands seemed palsied. He couldn't even navigate his own spoon.

Marla met in secret with a couple of high-priced fixers, known as shadow men in that netherworld of theirs, and she did what a daughter had to do. All the government witnesses "vaporized," as the shadow men had predicted. The case was dropped. But Daddy had a stroke.

Marla shut down Silk & Silk and sold whatever assets the company had. Her husband left her.

"Marla," he scribbled in a short note, "you let me dangle in the wind."

It wasn't as simple as that. She'd kept him in the dark because she didn't want Candice and Lollie Jr. to be the daughters of a jailbird. But Rafe hadn't been wrong. He wasn't a Silk, and she couldn't entrust her father's secrets to him. Rafe ran off with his own secretary, a cousin of Marla's. And she put Mortimer's thirty-room apartment on the market. Marla had to move Mortimer and Lollie into her own fifteen-room affair.

After having rescued her father from a court battle, where all the Silks would have been sullied, Marla was hired as the in-house lawyer at an arbitrage firm almost as grandiose as Silk & Silk had once been. She was thirty-seven now, and she began to paint her face white, like some Egyptian queen.

She couldn't even talk to her own girls, who would Twitter or tweet at the kitchen table and seemed part of some arcane universe where anyone over the age of fifteen had no right to exist. She was lonely. She had love affairs. None of the lawyers or brokers she met made much of an impression. She kept a room at the St. Regis under Mortimer's name, and that's where she had her "twitters and tweets," as she liked to call her little liaisons.

But Marla had problems at home. Mother was bereft without Rumpelmayer's, which had locked its doors forever, and Daddy wandered around in a tattered robe from his student years, one side of his face disfigured from the stroke.

Once every two or three months, Lollie would get lost in Central Park. It wasn't serious unless she was trapped in the middle of a snowstorm. Mother had her own nurse, but Marla wouldn't trust a paid companion to extricate Lollie from the snow. So she put on her galoshes and fur hat, left her midtown office in the middle of a meeting, and plunged into the park.

Mother didn't have a favorite bridge or tree, and Marla had to travel by instinct. She worried that Mother might fall and lie buried in the snow. But Marla always found her, as if she had some hidden radar. It was silence that was her real accomplice, the silence of the snow; it was as if she could hear the whole planet breathe while she traversed the park.

And there was Mother, sitting on a bench beside Belvedere Castle, with snow in her lap. Whipped by the wind, the huge snowflakes had begun to sting Marla's face.

"It's a pity," Mother said, playing with her mittens.

"Mummy," Marla said with a touch of bitterness, "if you keep talking, you'll get snow in your mouth—and I'll have to call an ambulance."

"It's a pity," Mother said, trying to light a cigarette in the wind. "If I had Rumpelmayer's, I wouldn't be on a park bench. Rumpelmayer's might have consoled me."

"Console you for what?"

"For having a daughter who's a whore."

Marla considered strangling Lollie and leaving her to drift in the snow.

"Constance Bengelman saw you at the King Cole Bar. The barman told her that you have a room at the St. Regis, and that you flirt with every sort of man who wears pants."

"And suppose I do?"

Marla was bewildered. Did Lollie have her own network of spies? Constance Bengelman must have been one of her former soul mates from Rumpelmayer's. "And suppose I do?"

"Then you're cheap, and I raised a daughter who's a common harlot."

"But you never raised me—Daddy did. And both of us raised you."

"That's unfair," Lollie said. "That's brutal. I'm a Kansas girl . . ."

"Just like Dorothy," Marla said. "In your favorite film. But I have no Cowardly Lion to lend you."

Lollie preened on her bench. "You shouldn't make fun of a widow."

And Marla realized she could never win—Mother knew how to wound with her melancholy.

"Your father's been dead to me for years. Even before his *accident*. I suppose he had his own little chippie at the St. Moritz. I shouldn't have married. My father warned me about becoming a Jewess."

It was the same old mad tale. "Mother, you've never been inside a synagogue in your life. And neither have I."

But Marla sensed that shrewdness in her mother's eyes, even behind a shield of snow.

"Didn't your father join Temple Emanu-El?"

"Did he have a choice? Half his clients were members of Emanu-El."

And Marla heard that purring voice out of the snow.

"Wasn't he going to give you a bas mitzvah . . . and cater it at the Pierre?"

Marla ruffled her nose. "Bas mitzvah? Isn't that where the rabbi cuts your clit?"

Both of them started to giggle among the falling flakes like a couple of schoolgirls. Mother was roaring with energy now, as if someone had stuffed her with celestial chimes. She began to march in the snow. Marla had the devil of a time keeping up with her.

She continued to haunt the St. Regis. Marla sat at the King Cole Bar with her glass of pinot noir, right under the Maxfield Parrish; Old King Cole looked like an idiot, surrounded by his own simpletons, his spectacles askew. Marla wondered if the king was half-blind; but the reds and browns in the mural, and the king's gold hat, seemed to warm Marla's bones on winter nights. She wasn't in the mood to rut with a man. And that's when she saw him. He was a few years younger than Marla; he had flecks of gray in his hair and a tiny scar near his mouth that she would have loved to lick. She couldn't even say why that scar had aroused her so. She'd seen him before, not at the St. Regis. He could have been a Yalie, since he was wearing a tie with the college seal. *It was at Silk & Silk*, that's where she had seen him. He'd worked for Daddy once upon a time.

He sat down next to Marla with all the confidence of King Cole. She liked that.

"I can have you arrested," she whispered in his ear.

He laughed. That scar near his mouth moved. "Would you handcuff me, Miss Marla?"

"I didn't give you the right to mention my name."

"Then what should I call you?"

"I forgot to bring my handcuffs," she hissed with a kind of soft venom. "You're not a Yalie, are you?"

"I went to Fordham," he said. "But Fordham doesn't leave much of an echo. It wouldn't get me near enough to smell your perfume."

"But you could have lied."

"I think you've had enough Yalies in your life. . . . What should I call you?"

"Miss Marla," she said.

They went up to her room. He was tender with her . . . and brutal, pretending to handcuff himself while he pinned her to the bed. She couldn't stop running her fingers through his scalp. She was the idiot now, Old Queen Cole, who fell in love with some high-class gigolo, because it was love, and nothing less than that.

"My father fired you, didn't he?"

"Yes, he did, Miss Marla."

"You were gone in a flash. That much I do remember."

"He would have forgiven anything if I had been a Silk. We grew up in the same Bronx neighborhood."

"What are you talking about?"

"He'd lived at the Lewis Morris—I lived there many years later, when it was more like a jail, with wire mesh in the windows to keep out the burglars and the addicts. We liked to reminisce. That's why he hired me. I didn't have much of a résumé. I was lucky to get out of Fordham alive."

"And then he fired you."

"I went through all his female executives like a crazy scythe."

"Then why didn't you get to me . . . with the same scythe?"

"Ah," he said with a gorgeous smile. "I have one cardinal rule: Never touch the boss's daughter."

His last name was Banderas, like the movie star who was married to Melanie Griffith. His first name was Raoul. They met at the St. Regis almost every night, dined at the bar. At first he wouldn't take any cash from her. But she insisted.

"Indulge me," she said. "Use it as pocket money to replenish your wardrobe with another Yale tie."

"But I might strangle you with it if you make fun of me, Miss Marla."

"That would be perfect—to come before I croaked."

She would traipse home at one in the morning in her million-dollar pumps from Louboutin and find Lollie sitting there like a bulldog.

"You've abandoned your own girls."

Lollie knew how to blind her daughter with a few choice barbs. But Marla wouldn't let Lollie catch her with blood in her eyes.

"They can always Twitter me if they're in trouble."

"You're heartless," Lollie said.

"No, I'm crazy about a man."

Marla had no one to talk to about her own Antonio Banderas. But she did ask Mortimer to accompany her into the Bronx and show her where the Silks had once resided. He was forlorn in his tattered robe. But he relished being in a limo, and his good humor came back. They traveled up to the Concourse. The Lewis Morris resembled a Park Avenue palace that had fallen into ruin. Part of its front wall seemed as if it had been burnt or been lately under siege. Its doorman had a bulletproof vest.

Daddy had a blank look on the damaged side of his face. The stroke had ravaged him, but some fire still must have burned inside his skull. And suddenly he wasn't ravaged at all.

"Marla, once upon a time, dentists would kill for a suite at the Lewis Morris."

They rode down a hill to a tiny Italian ghetto with its own ducal restaurant, where the waiters welcomed Daddy in his robe. They served him dish after dish, with tiny glasses of red wine. Marla ate whatever Daddy ate. Finally she mentioned Raoul.

"He's probably a confidence man, but I don't care. Why did you fire him?"

She could feel him wander through all that rubble in his head. The bad side of his face began to twitch.

"I never fired anyone named Raoul."

"You talked with him about the Bronx—and the Lewis Morris. Daddy, Raoul looks like Antonio Banderas."

The clam sauce had spilled under Mortimer's napkin—Marla wouldn't wipe her own father, as if he were a deranged orphan at the restaurant. But there was a boy's mischief in his eye.

"Does he have a little scar under his mouth—almost like an unhealed scratch?"

"Yes!" She gripped Mortimer's arm so fiercely, he started to blanch.

"He moved in with one of our bookkeepers, beat up her boys, and threatened to kill them if she didn't hand over her paycheck—every month. He held one of her boys halfway out the window. Gabriel, that's the name he used. And he wasn't from the Bronx."

"How come you never told me about this Gabriel?"

The mischief was still there in Daddy's eye. "Tell you what? That he was the lord and master of our copy machines? The detectives who came looking for him said he was some customer. He set a man on fire in Miami."

Marla ran home to her little girls, who weren't so little anymore. Candice and Lollie Jr. thought she was insane when she tried to hug them for a whole minute.

"Mother," Candice said, "you're wrinkling my blouse."

But Marla adored their complaints, even adored their texting and Twittering—that electric quality of their lives, where one minute morphed into another with its own maniacal message.

She couldn't confront Raoul. He would only have lied and lied until she weakened and licked his scar again. She met with the same team that had "solved" Daddy's other problems, had scared off the witnesses in his court case. She'd never asked these shadow men about their methods, but this time she did.

"I don't want him hurt—just frightened to death, so he'll never come near me or my girls."

They must have been ex-soldiers. They had the straightest backs she had ever seen. That's what she liked about them. They had their own touch of class. She told them about her next rendezvous at the St. Regis. She paid the shadow men in hundred-dollar bills.

"Mrs. Silk," they said, "just you rest up. It will be done."

She hadn't bothered to change her name, even when she was married. Candice and Lollie Jr. were Silks, just like her.

"You won't hurt him?"

"Not a hair on his head."

She panicked, wanted to call Raoul and tell him to run. But she knew the consequences. Raoul might have stalked her, sat at the bar, right under King Cole in his funny crown, like a lunatic's thinking cap.

She kept away from the St. Regis, though she continued to rent the room. It made her feel mysterious. Six months passed.

She had to rescue Lollie one more time from the clutches of Central Park. She played pinochle with her father whenever she had a free moment. She hired a tutor to help Candice and Lollie Jr. with their homework and thanked God they hadn't been harmed by that maniac who'd set fire to a man in Miami. And she threw herself into her own work. She was named a senior vice president and decided to celebrate with a glass of pinot noir at the St. Regis.

Marla sat in her old chair, right under the reds, browns, and blues of Maxfield Parrish. She paid no attention to the yattering around her. She looked at the bottles of Courvoisier behind the bar. And it was as if she'd conjured him up from a dream. There he was in his Yale tie, with bruises under his cheekbone.

"Miss Marla, I told the barman that your drink was on the house. Old King Cole is as happy to see you as I am."

He hesitated, didn't sit down at first. She couldn't stop peeking at the scar near his mouth. Daddy had been right. It did look like an inflamed scratch.

She'd finished half her pinot noir, and she could afford to play the conjurer. She beckoned Gabriel-Raoul to sit beside her.

"Congratulations," he said. "Your hirelings knew how to be delicate. They could have broken my face, but they didn't."

Marla wanted to lick all his wounds and shout that she was sorry.

"You shouldn't have followed me here," she said.

"I wasn't following you, Miss Marla. This is my watering hole. I sit here like a monk and commune with King Cole."

"Whenever you're not setting fire to someone or hanging little boys outside a window."

The wound near his mouth seemed to leap out of its own carapace, like some living creature.

"I should slap your face," he said.

"I'll kill you if you come near my children."

She started to cry. She didn't even have much of a revelation. Daddy had hid behind one of his Marrano masks—he'd lied about Raoul.

She stood up and meandered up to her room, with that fugitive from Miami right behind her. She would have welcomed a beating. She's the one who had been bad. But Raoul was as tender with her as he had ever been. Marla was confused. She wanted to be spanked. Then he wrapped his Yale necktie around her neck. *Good*, she thought. *It will be the end of me.*

But he made love to her with that necktie around her neck, as if she were Yale's homecoming queen. Marla couldn't believe that he'd set fire to a man. She traced the scars on his chest with her little finger. But she had to declare her own independence from him before she was swallowed up in that wonderful map of his skin.

"Raoul, or whatever your name is, how many men did you murder in Miami?"

He smiled, and all her gruffness went away.

"Miss Marla, I couldn't even tell you what Miami looks like."

"Father says you were in charge of the copy machine."

He was no longer smiling. "Yeah, I *was* his copying machine."

"Don't be so damn cryptic," she spat at him. She was donning her very own mask. If Marla didn't get away from Raoul and the St. Regis, she would be ruined.

"I looked after his mistresses," he said.

"What mistresses?"

"Why do you think I got that cozy with the St. Regis? Mr. Mortimer kept his own suite."

"I don't believe it," Marla said. But she did believe it. That's the kind of secret Daddy would have.

"Some were call girls," Raoul said. "I'd entertain them until Mr. Mortimer arrived. Some were fashion designers and models who needed an extra buck. Your father wasn't interested in romance. I did most of his courting."

"Stop it," Marla said. "You were Mortimer's pimp."

"No," Raoul said. "I never chose his mistresses. I amused them."

"And took them up to my father's room."

She raged with jealousy as she imagined the tight little bodies of the models and the Rubenesque proportions of the prostitutes—their ample arms, breasts that could smother Raoul.

"That's why I got canned. He said I made him look small, that he couldn't tantalize these women after they had been with me."

"And what happened when I walked into the King Cole that first time?"

"I was confused. The barmen told me you had your own room. And I figured that Mr. Mortimer had sent you, and that you were looking for a scout."

She glared at him. "Why would I need the services of a scout?"

"To help you fish for men."

She wanted to pluck out his eyes. But Marla played the diplomat.

"How delicate you are! But I don't need barmen or scouts. I need you."

Ah, if she could only have another glass of wine. She didn't know what to do with Raoul. Should she shower money at him, like she did with those shadow men who couldn't even scare him off? Should Marla keep him like a poodle? But she was the poodle, despite her bank account.

"I'll give you a thousand dollars if you spend the night with me—that's what I pay for my shoes."

He tightened his tie around her windpipe, but even that violence in him was gentle. Marla was lost. He whispered in her ear.

"If you mention money one more time, I will set you on fire."

She started to cry, but it was the noiseless whimper of a little girl. She could have phoned the nighttime nurse who looked after Lollie and Mortimer, or even Twittered her two girls. They could survive without a mother, at least for one night. She'd never bothered to bring pajamas to the St. Regis. Marla's room had the same soft glow as the King Cole Bar. She could see the outline of Raoul. His eyes seemed to burn in the dark—she loved that dancing, electric dark of the King Cole. She hummed to herself as Raoul wiped her tears with a finger that had the miraculous touch of velvet fur. *Lord*, as Lollie would say, *I have myself a man*. What did she care if Daddy's detectives came for her tomorrow? Daddy didn't have detectives. He had to negotiate each step to the toilet.

Let him tumble. She wouldn't run home to him. Marla was spending the night with Raoul.

LITTLE SISTER

Whatever Marla did, Marla did so well. The golden spoon she'd been born with had never failed her, but her little sister had gagged on the same spoon. Little Sister wasn't so little. She was a twelve-pound baby who inherited most of Marla's toys. When she couldn't solve their intricate engines, Marla would have to be called in. Little Sister had a name, but no one seemed to recollect it. She'd turn glum or fall into terrible fits. She struck Marla with a shoe when she was three and Marla was four.

She was banished to a back bedroom in the family's palatial apartment on Central Park West. Soon she had her own guardian, and Marla seldom saw her. When Marla was five, Little Sister disappeared from the apartment. Soon Marla began to feel as if she'd never really had a sister, but had been visited by some strange goblin or ghost.

Little Sister was never mentioned at the dinner table. There were no pictures of her in the apartment. The back bedroom was turned into a storage bin, but a lock was on the door, and Marla couldn't get in. Her father, Mortimer Silk, was the arbitrage king of Wall Street. He made fortunes on the rise and fall of currencies and was the commander of his own "frigate," as he liked to call his firm. Her mother, Lollie, had been the homecoming queen at Ohio State. And whenever Marla had a jolt in her mind and mentioned Little Sister, Lollie would ruffle her nose.

"Dearest, I haven't the slightest idea what you're talking about. You have no sister."

Marla wouldn't pester Daddy, because he was so sensitive and might have started to cry. So she interrogated the doormen. They looked at her as if she had seen her own goblin in the elevator.

"We can't help you, Miss Marla."

She lived with that goblin, grew up with it, and when she graduated from Columbia Law, she volunteered for duty aboard her father's frigate. Within a year she was chief counsel at Silk & Silk. She married her high school sweetheart, had two children, and lived in the same apartment-palace on Central Park West.

Mortimer died before he was sixty. Marla cleaned up all the mess. And while going through her father's safety deposit boxes she found the first hard evidence of Little Sister. Daddy hadn't abandoned her. Sister's real name was Irene. Mortimer had put her in a home for alcoholic movie stars and mental patients on an isolated block near the Bronx Botanical Garden. Mortimer had kept a record of every transaction with Rhineland Manor, like a ship captain's log. He'd visited Little Sister every second week, set up an account for her in perpetuity. Marla wouldn't have uncovered a single clue if she hadn't gone into the vault at Daddy's bank. Irene wasn't even mentioned in Mortimer's will.

She ran home with all the records, confronted Lollie. Marla ranted for an hour, but Lollie didn't blink once, didn't falter under Marla's attack.

"We did what was best," Lollie insisted. "She tried to smother you with a pillow while you were asleep. Little Sister was an aberrant child."

"Mummy, Little Sister has a name—Irene."

"You mustn't shout," Lollie said. "No one ever called her Irene."

Marla decided not to tell her children until she had gone up to see Little Sister for herself. She'd become chief counsel at another arbitrage firm, and she had the company chauffeur drive her into the wild lands of the Bronx. What she saw wasn't so wild. Rhineland Manor was in a neighborhood of Tudor-style apartment houses. The mansion itself had once been a cloister for decrepit nuns and was surrounded by a sculpted garden.

Marla had a hard time getting through the mansion's gates. It meant nothing that she was her father's executor and one of his heirs. Little Sister wasn't insane and could decide for herself whom she wanted to see.

Marla could have gone to court, but she wasn't going to sue the mansion and Little Sister. And there was another problem about Irene. She would answer to no name but Bunny.

"I'm sorry, Mrs. Silk," the chief nurse said. "Bunny says she has no sister."

Marla didn't have to discard her husband's name. She was always known as Mrs. Silk. And she was just as stubborn as Little Sister.

"Then I guess I'll have a very long wait. And even if my father has paid Bunny's upkeep for the rest of her natural life, I'll dig right into his estate and ask to have that money returned. So you may have a pauper on your hands."

The nurses whispered among themselves, and then Bunny appeared. She had broad shoulders, looked like a man. Marla could sense the rage in her. Perhaps Lollie hadn't made up that tale about Little Sister trying to smother her with a pillow.

Something was wrong with Bunny's eyes. They seemed to wander even as they took Marla in. There was a pulse between her eyebrows, like some strange target. Marla wasn't sure how to introduce herself.

"I'm your sister," she said.

"I don't remember you," Bunny said. Her voice wasn't tentative. But it didn't have the lilt of Manhattan. Marla couldn't trace the accent. Little Sister could have been the soprano of Rhineland Manor and the Bronx Botanical Garden.

"But Daddy visited you every other week. He must have told you about . . ."

Marla couldn't even finish her sentence. Mortimer had told Little Sister nothing about the Silks.

Bunny smiled. "He called himself Uncle Mort. He took me on excursions . . . and he paid for all my tutors. I couldn't sit in a classroom with other kids. No school would have me. I destroyed the first classroom I was in. Ripped out every seat. . . . Why the hell are you here?"

"Bunny, I found—"

"Don't call me that," Little Sister said. Her eyes had a yellow gleam. The smile was gone, replaced by a wolf's grin. "That's for my friends. Uncle called me Irene. You know, from that song, 'Goodnight, Irene.' He sang it to me all the time, said he'd see me in his dreams."

Marla was filled with her own rage, not against Little Sister, but against Mortimer, who hadn't serenaded her once.

"And he cried a lot, said he couldn't take me with him, because no insurance policy in the whole world could guard against a danger like me."

"Daddy didn't say that."

"Yes, he did," Bunny said, smiling again. The dentists around Rhineland Manor couldn't have been so perfect—she had missing teeth. And then her accent started to crumble; she sounded like the gang leader of some housing project in the neighborhood. "Listen, girl, I'm not that stupid. I'm in this dump because of you. I'll rip your tits out, like the sockets on a chair."

Two male nurses arrived and led Bunny upstairs to the living quarters, while Marla was summoned to the directress's office, where a certain Mrs. Mahler was waiting. The directress seemed about fifty. She served Marla coffee in a beautiful cup.

"I suppose I'm a pain in the ass," Marla said. "An intruder."

"Not at all," Mrs. Mahler said. "It happens all the time. A relative hidden away, not entirely for medical reasons. No one's under lock and key."

"But I thought my sister was violent. Didn't she tear up her own school?"

"She had a tantrum. But we kept a nurse in the class, you see. And your father chose a better arrangement. He hired a bunch of sophomores from Fordham University. It was quite convenient. Fordham's ten blocks away. The students liked to come here, and your sister received a fine education."

"Did my father pick the tutors himself?"

"Indeed. Often he was here every other day."

Marla couldn't hide the shudder that leapt right through her. *Every other day.* She had to keep herself from asking if Daddy had his own bed at this mansion. She took out her checkbook and began to scribble a check. Mrs. Mahler seemed perplexed.

"We can't accept money from you, Mrs. Silk."

"A few extras," Marla said. "In case my sister shatters one of your coffee cups."

"But it's forbidden."

"Forbidden by whom?" Marla had to ask.

"Your father. He didn't want Bunny to become a burden. He's endowed this home, you see, and we stand to lose that endowment if the financial arrangement for his daughter is tampered with or compromised in any way."

Marla began to wonder if the directress had her own law degree from Fordham. She didn't argue. She thanked Mrs. Mahler and said she wouldn't trouble her or Little Sister again.

But her anger turned to bile. Mortimer had shut her out, denied

Marla the rights to her own little sister. She had her chauffeur drive from the Botanical Garden to the Madison Avenue offices of her father's lawyer. She gave Martin Goodson, Esq., fifteen minutes of warning. But when Marla arrived in Goodson's own office, all the senior partners were there. Goodson was a portly man who wrote novels in his spare time. He'd never cheated Mortimer out of a nickel.

"Martin," she said, "I'd like to see the codicil to my father's will."

"The will didn't have one, Marla."

"Then I'll subpoena all your records. I'm Dad's executor, not you."

Goodson motioned to his partners, and they all left the room.

"If Daddy set up an endowment, I'm going to claim he wasn't in his right mind. I don't trust that shyster home in the Bronx. It smacks of a prison."

"Marla, did you know that your mother and father once had a wolf?"

She should have been furious, with her father's lawyer going off on some tangent like that. But it pricked her imagination. "What wolf?"

"A Siberian wolf-dog with a white coat and silver eyes. They called her Princess. She was the envy of your father's building. And she was devoted to Mort, terribly devoted. That white wolf would only eat from your father's hand."

A she-wolf with silver eyes on Central Park West. Marla had a horrible premonition.

"Then I was born," she said. "And the wolf was jealous."

"She attacked the doormen. Mort had to put her away."

Marla had two daughters in their teens. They would text at the dinner table, text while they brushed their teeth. They loved Marla but considered her a relic from some century without tweets. So it was futile to mention a maiden aunt.

But it was Lollie who read the sad lines on her daughter's brow.

"You went up to see that maniac, didn't you?"

"Mummy, she's not a maniac. She's a prisoner in a golden cage. But why didn't you tell me about the wolf?"

Now it was Lollie who had that fierce pulse between her eyes. "Princess wasn't a wolf. Your father couldn't be consoled. He wept for days."

And soon Marla could weave in all the particulars of the tale. Daddy had to make a second sacrifice, give up another she-wolf, Little Sister, who had rages he couldn't control. He tried and tried, with a little army of specialists and shamans. But they must have come to the same conclusion: the wolf cub couldn't live at home, or Marla's life might have been in mortal danger. So they found a way to "gas" Little Sister and keep her alive.

And Marla had become a kind of golem whose husband had left her for his secretary. No, she was a succubus who fed from afar on Little Sister's blood. She thought of resigning her job. She had love affairs with silly men. A succubus might as well feed on someone's blood.

Then she got a call from Rhineland Manor. Little Sister wanted to see her. Marla borrowed the same chauffeur and company car.

She could hardly believe the transformation. Bunny's hair was longer. Her shoulders were tucked in. She wore pumps and a silk blouse. Most of her masculinity was gone. They sat on the mansion's verandah, could listen to the lions in the Bronx Zoo. Bunny didn't have the musk of a prisoner. She served coffee in a silver tray. They had almond biscuits from an Italian bakery on Arthur Avenue.

"I'm shameless," Bunny said. "I put on a big act. . . . Do you know how many times I dreamt of sitting here with you?"

"But you could have asked Uncle Mort to bring me along. I would have come. . . . Did he ever talk about me?"

"Sometimes. But he never said we were sisters."

Daddy wanted to keep Little Sister in a grandiose closet. He didn't have to talk about money and ambition with her, about arbitrage . . .

And then a thought seized Marla. "Did Daddy ever mention his wolf-dog, Princess?"

Suddenly Little Sister's eyes were flecked with wild spots. She began to mold an almond biscuit in her hand. She looked like some axe murderer in her silk blouse.

"That was his pet name for me—Princess. He took me there . . ."

"*There*," Marla muttered.

"He put up a marker after Princess died. He had a tiny gravestone dug into the earth, in Central Park."

"I don't believe you," Marla said. It was a fabrication, a vast plot to rob Marla of whatever tranquillity she had left. There was no such creature as Princess, no wolf-dog with a white coat, no matter what Daddy had told his lawyer, or what Lollie had said. Lollie always lied. No wolf had been put to sleep on Marla's account.

"I don't believe you . . . about the marker."

Little Sister clutched Marla's hand; Marla thought the bones in her fingers would break. But she didn't squeal.

"Uncle Mort had a pair of silver eyes painted on it."

Marla thought she would swoon. Little Sister released her hand. And Marla fled the mansion like a half-crazed vagabond.

Marla was caught in a maelstrom and a widening mesh. She dreamt of wolf-dogs in Central Park. Winter came, and she would wander about after every snowfall, sometimes in the midst of a storm. But she didn't neglect her court cases. She had a wolf's silver eyes in court. Lawyers were frightened to sue her firm. Marla would tear witnesses apart, Marla went for the throat. But she wouldn't visit Little Sister again, wouldn't make those excursions across the Henry Hudson Bridge. The Bronx fell out of her dreams.

Then she had a visitor at her office on Lexington Avenue—two visitors. They had come uninvited. But Marla couldn't send her own sister away. Bunny was wearing a coat of Siberian fur. The man with her was in some kind of uniform. Marla had seen him before. He was the gardener at Rhineland Manor.

Marla didn't know how to behave. She'd never had Little Sister in her office, and with a male gardener. She summoned her male secretary from his cubicle and had him fetch cups of coffee and little cakes from the firm's own kitchen. She had Bunny and the gardener sit on the black leather couch beside her own desk. Bunny wouldn't take off her coat.

"Sis," she said, "we're getting married."

Marla felt a tug in her throat. This gardener hadn't made much of an impression. His hair wasn't combed. He couldn't even shave correctly. He had the beginnings of a mustache. And he was much younger than the heiress of Rhineland Manor.

"Bunny, aren't you going to introduce me to your fiancé?"

"Sis, meet Roger Blunt. He was one of my tutors."

Marla shuddered at the sound of that name. *Roger Blunt*. But he had the bluest eyes in all of Manhattan . . . and the Bronx. That was a conniver's color—no, it was the camouflage of a seducer.

"I was hopeless without Roger, Sis, couldn't even have a conversation. He calmed me down, taught me how to converse with other human beings."

Marla had to be careful around this Roger Blunt. "Bunny," she said, "gardeners at convalescent homes don't often become tutors."

Little Sister was growing agitated; that pulse between her eyes reappeared.

"Rog's no gardener. That's temporary. Mrs. Mahler had him sent over from Fordham. He was a divinity student. That's what attracted me. He was close to God."

Marla couldn't suppress her lawyer's instincts. "Why isn't he a divinity student now?"

She knew she was playing with fire. Roger Blunt didn't have to come here in a gardener's uniform. He wanted to provoke Marla, frighten her even. Little Sister slumped in her seat and began to whimper.

"Bunny," Marla said, "I . . ."

The gardener's malicious smile cut her off.

"Mrs. Silk," he said, in his own silken voice. "Bunny's what the staff and the other patients decided to call Irene, to keep her a child. But she's thirty-seven years old. She has the right to be Irene."

"I'm sorry," Marla said.

The gardener must have studied up on state law. Little Sister hadn't been written out of Daddy's will. Daddy just wanted to keep her hidden. And so this secret sister stood to inherit half of whatever Marla had inherited. And Roger Blunt pounced on Marla with his blue eyes.

"I dropped out of divinity school. And the home was kind enough to hire me. I'd been a gardener before."

"Roger," Marla said, mustering as much silk as she could. "How much will you need?"

"A hundred thousand dollars."

Marla laughed to herself. Roger Blunt wasn't even trying to burgle Daddy's will. He just wanted little pieces of Marla's flesh. She had a mad urge to write a check and get rid of him. He'd cash it and run away to some other badland. And Little Sister would mourn him the rest of her life.

"And where will both of you live?"

"In the Bronx. Moving somewhere else would unsettle Irene. She knows every squirrel in Bronx Park. I have a room in the attic. Mrs. Mahler has agreed to let me live there—until we're married."

"And is the hundred thousand for a wedding party?"

Little Sister started to guffaw. "We had the party, Sis. At Rhineland . . . it would have been a lot less fun *after* the wedding."

"That money is to pay my bills," said Roger Blunt. "I owe Fordham a ton."

Marla tapped a button on her phone: it was a signal to her secretary, who knocked, and entered. "You're wanted in the conference room, Mrs. Silk."

"Irene, I'll be right back."

She dialed Mrs. Mahler from another office and was quite severe once the directress came to the phone.

"Mrs. Mahler, what the hell is going on? Are you in the habit of hiring charlatans and gigolos as your gardener?"

There was complete silence, and Marla assumed she had lost the connection. Then Mrs. Mahler's voice broke through that silence.

"He is a charlatan. But Rog brought Bunny back from the dead."

Marla raged. Her shoulders puffed out. She began plotting strategies to shut the convalescent home.

"Mahler, do we have to bring melodrama to the table? If my sister was so ill, why didn't you inform me?"

"You forget, Mrs. Silk. I'm forbidden to call any member of the family. That was in our covenant with your father. Oh, we did have a doctor from Bronx-Lebanon. He gave her some vitamin B shots. But she still couldn't get out of bed. And then Rog started reading poems to her. He chanted them, really. He'd been her tutor."

"What kind of poems?" Marla asked, like some special prosecutor.

"I can't remember. I wouldn't listen in. But they were poems you might have in a high school curriculum. Joyce Kilmer and George Pope Morris—you know, 'Woodman, spare that tree.' She adored poems about trees."

Marla returned to her office and wrote a check for a hundred thousand dollars. She didn't touch the fiduciary fund from her father's estate. Marla tapped into her own private account. She disliked the smell of victory that seemed to waft right from the gardener's stale clothes. She didn't care. The gardener could go to hell. Little Sister rose up from the couch and kissed Marla on the cheek.

"Now you're looking after me, Sis. Tell me what Uncle Mort said every time he had to leave—*tell me!*"

Marla didn't even have to guess. "Goodnight, Irene."

She'd landed in the middle of a plague. She dreamt of this gardener with his slick blue eyes. None of her lovers could satisfy her now; even when they licked the life out of her, she kept seeing those blue eyes. She was miserable. She thought of hiring her two shadow men, those fixers who had kept Mortimer out of jail after he'd been indicted for tax evasion. These shadow men had managed to scatter all the government's witnesses. But what could they do about Roger Blunt? Little Sister's life seemed to depend on him.

There were no more demands for money, no more visits from the lovebirds.

She thought about visiting them, planned her voyage in the company car, even imagined crossing Spuyten Duyvil Creek on the Henry Hudson, seeing that narrow woodland at the very edge of Inwood Hill Park. But she couldn't seem to manage the trip, consumed as she was by some dread that made her shiver half the night.

Then she got a call from the convalescent home. She sailed across Spuyten Duyvil Creek in the company car, rushed through the gate at Rhineland Manor. Mrs. Mahler met her on the front porch.

"Did that charlatan abscond with the money?" she asked. "Mahler, it doesn't matter. I'll lure him back with an even bigger net. My sister won't have to suffer."

"My dear," Mrs. Mahler said, "the problem is much more serious than that. It seems our charlatan already has a wife—and two toddlers. And he's moved with them to Montana, or Delaware. I'm not certain."

Marla leapt upstairs to her sister's room. She'd never seen Rhineland's inner sanctum. Sister's bedroom was quite small, with very simple furniture, but the rear wall was cluttered with photographs, and Marla was wounded by the sight of them. Her whole damn history was on that wall: snapshots of Sister when she was one and Marla was two; shots of them a few years later, Sister hovering over Marla, like a little giant with a look of rampant rage; shots of Sister with the guardian Daddy had hired for her; shots of Sister in Central Park; but nothing of Sister after that. The rest of the wall was devoted to Marla and Marla's two daughters: Marla in her graduation gown, Marla on a trip to Tunis with her husband, Marla touring Lisbon as she looked for her father's Marrano ancestors, Marla at Silk & Silk, Marla at her new firm—Marla, Marla everywhere. And hidden among this tapestry was an old, tattered picture of Mortimer's Siberian wolf-dog; Princess's face was obscured, but not her white coat and one diamond-pure eye.

Marla couldn't keep from sobbing. She sat down on Sister's bed. Irene had lost her hulking look. Her eyes were full of fever. Her shoulders were as narrow and delicate as a little girl's.

"Irene," she whispered, "I'll find Roger Blunt. I'll send his wife and two kids to China."

"I'm sorry I tricked you, Sis. That money was never for us. I knew about Rog's wife. They were in trouble. He didn't have enough to feed his family."

"Then you weren't in love with the gardener?"

"I was. A little. We kissed and played around. And he sang songs to me."

"'Goodnight, Irene.'"

"No," she said. "That was between Uncle Mort and me."

"But why did Daddy give you all those pictures to decorate your wall?"

Sister stared at Marla with her fevered eyes. "Because I wanted them. I begged. I had tantrums."

Marla touched her sister's face for the first time. And she was the one who needed comfort now; she'd been Daddy's accomplice when she should have screamed and screamed and gotten her sister back.

It was Marla's fault. Never mind a phantom wolf-dog. Marla had sucked up all the air around her. Daddy wasn't protecting Marla from Irene. He was preserving Little Sister from Marla's rapaciousness, hiding Sister in their Bronx retreat.

Little Sister started to cough. Marla wiped her mouth with a handkerchief. But something scratched at Marla.

"Sister, why did you pretend not to know me when I came here that first time?"

"I was scared. I kept looking at you and your kids on my wall. I ripped off their shoulders in my dreams."

"Good," Marla said. "Then you won't have to rip off their shoulders when you all meet."

Little Sister laughed. A doctor arrived from Bronx-Lebanon with an ambulance attendant. The doctor wore a turban. He might have been a Sikh. They must have come in a great hurry.

They'd forgotten to bring a stretcher. So they carried Little Sister down the stairs in her own camp bed while Marla held her hand.

"I'll stay with you in the hospital, I swear," Marla shouted into the woodwork. "We'll live in the same room."

Little Sister coughed and breathed in great little gasps when they arrived at the bottom of the stairs. "Sis," she said, shutting her eyes, "see you in my dreams."

And Marla whispered "Goodnight, goodnight, Irene," while the doctor and the attendant carried Little Sister out the door and into the ambulance.

MARLA

1.

Lollie blinked when Marla brought Little Sister home from Rhineland Manor.

She devoured Irene with a murderous glare. "Who is this stranger?"

"Mother," Marla said, "be quiet."

She could handle Lollie—bribe her if she had to—but she was less certain about her own teenage daughters, Candice and Lollie Jr. Could they cope with a *stranger* in the house, an aunt they had never even heard of? There was plenty of space for Irene. The Silks lived in fifteen rooms on Central Park West. Marla had just moved to a larger law firm—Bregman, Bourne, soon to be Bregman, Bourne & Silk.

But Marla needn't have worried about Candice and Lollie Jr.—they adopted Irene, like some pet snake.

"Awesome," they said. "We have a new aunt."

Candice and Lollie Jr. bragged about Irene, brought her up to their school in Riverdale, had her pose half-naked in their art classes. Marla knew the girls would tire of Irene, but she could only deal with one crisis at a time. She worked sixteen-hour days at Bregman, Bourne & Silk. Prosecutors in all five boroughs were reluctant to meet Marla in open court—she massacred their most reliable witnesses. Whatever case they built, Marla tore it down. She had the finest investigators in the business, a pair of shadow men who had kept her father out of jail. They had a military background and must have graduated from some super-secret agency.

When they appeared at Bregman, Bourne & Silk, the senior partners shut their doors. There was nothing salacious or shifty about these shadow men. They wore identical suits from Brooks Brothers—charcoal gray with a hint of green—and identical ties. Their shoes were made of Spanish leather. No one knew where they'd come from. They might have been cousins or brothers. Their faces had a slight bluish cast, as if they were once fond of wearing war paint. They were known as Marla's Indians.

Other law firms hoped to hire them away. But these shadow men—Hector and Paul—were loyal to Marla. They volunteered to squire Irene around—took her ice-skating at the Chelsea Piers, visited Ellis Island and the sculpted debris of the World Trade Center, went to Brighton Beach, where Irene wandered on the boardwalk and performed a few tricks with a little gang of Russian acrobats.

She dressed like a cowgirl in leather pants. And she slipped into some kind of life on Central Park West. Marla gave her a generous allowance, like she did with Candice and Lollie Jr. And she held on to one of her father's last rituals, a Sunday brunch at home. Her daughters had opted out of that ritual—they wouldn't *dream* of spending Sunday mornings with their own mother and Grandma Lollie. But at least Lollie didn't hide in her room. She played the martyr and sat with Irene.

Lollie would eat in silence for ten minutes. Irene had impeccable manners; she never licked her fingers, the way Lollie did. It was always Irene who broke the ice. She would talk about the alcoholic movie stars she had met at Rhineland Manor; Marla had never heard of a single one—Marisa Endicott, Gracie Chance . . .

"Oh, Gracie had a fling with Leonardo DiCaprio—Leo was the love of her life. They just happened to bump into each other on the set of *Titanic*."

Lollie came out from behind the little church she had made of her fingers. "I saw that film eleven times. I know every actor and actress by heart. There was no such creature as Gracie Chance in *Titanic*."

Irene plucked on the leather frills of her cowgirl coat. "She was Kate Winslet's body double. If you look hard enough, you can find her hands and feet."

"That's a lie," Lollie said, munching on some Russian coffee cake. She arched her neck like the homecoming queen at Ohio State—she considered everything after that her great fall; marriage, children, grandchildren meant very little. She reminded Marla of some brittle, half-mad bird of prey.

"Look at her! Your sister is seething. She cannot listen to the truth. I nearly died delivering her. She was seventeen pounds. I ought to be in the *Guinness Book of Records*. It's a miracle I survived that birth."

"Stop that," Marla said. "Stop that right now. Irene wasn't seventeen pounds."

"And how would you know, Miss Smarty-Pants? Were you in the delivery room with me? The nurse fainted. I had to push and push. I ruptured a million blood vessels. My face was splattered with her rotten blood."

Irene laughed and cut into the lox. "Mummy, I wish I had never come out."

"Don't call me that. It's disgusting. I'm not your mummy. I never was. You were a monster I had to expel from my loins. I never recovered, and I never will."

Lollie hurled her napkin at Little Sister and left the table. Marla clutched Irene's hand.

"We have a crazy mother. We always did. I don't know how Daddy put up with her . . . I do know. He never listened to more than *half* of what she had to say."

"But I could be the crazy one. Otherwise they wouldn't have locked me up."

"No one locked you up," Marla said, in a frenzied whisper. "Daddy stole you from us."

2.

Marla was suspicious of all the savage tales she heard, that Irene had been ungovernable as a child, had beaten Marla senseless with one of Lollie's shoes—or was it a hairbrush?—when she was three and a half. And they had to get rid of the little demon and put her in a gilded jail. It was like Franz Kafka on Central Park West, morbid doings behind a respectable screen. Marla didn't believe a word of it. She traversed the huge apartment, which wrapped around two corners, with its terra-cotta façade, and landed in Lollie's bedroom. Marla didn't even bother to knock. She didn't have to be polite with the homecoming queen.

Lollie had a panoramic view of the park, with the reservoir like a huge, oval emerald in the blazing sun. It was her widow's quarters, her fiefdom, with a sunken alcove where Lollie could dream in her facial masks and pretty herself without a purpose. But Marla shouldn't have been so cruel. She lived a monstrous life, shielding murderers and swindlers, defying prosecutors and ripping out the threads of their elaborate tales. "The girl has the biggest pair of balls in Manhattan." That's what the district attorney's men said about Marla Silk.

None of her liaisons ever lasted more than a couple of weeks. Perhaps Marla, and not her mother, was the half-mad bird of prey.

Lollie lay in bed reading one of the Modern Library classics she'd kept from Ohio State. From the fatness of the book, Marla figured it was Tolstoy.

"Mother, you have to stop *landing* on Irene."

Lollie glanced up from her book and hurled off her glasses with a sweep of her hand; she didn't want anyone, including her daughter, to know that she couldn't decipher a word without her reading glasses.

"Then she shouldn't lie about actresses who don't even exist. Gracie Chance, indeed."

Irene was a casualty of some civil war Marla still didn't understand.

"But she isn't the only liar in this house."

"Marla, don't speak in riddles. I'll have one of my migraines, and it will be your fault if I collapse."

"I suppose Irene's some vagabond I brought back from the Bronx."

"Oh, she's a vagabond, all right—a little, scheming vagabond. She seduced your father with her big brown eyes. He was attracted to her from the moment she was born. I was covered with blood and he cooed at her. It was almost fatal, a borderline case."

"Mother, do you have to be so damn melodramatic? I don't—"

"I wasn't the only one with jealous fits. You couldn't bear Irene and her big eyes."

"I don't believe you," Marla said, but why was she shivering? She never panicked in court. Marla could outstare judges and juries, could drive hostile witnesses half-insane, and now she shivered in Lollie's bedroom, with that enormous emerald eye outside the window.

"She hit you with one of my stiletto heels—again and again. She broke my best pair of shoes, the little bitch. Your skull was on fire. I told you how to play dead. And Irene stopped talking."

"Mummy, I don't understand."

"She turned mute—she had murder in her eyes."

Marla flared up with anger, could have slapped Lollie. "Shame on you," she said. "Having a four-year-old girl as an accomplice."

"You were almost five."

The doctors came, Lollie said. They examined Irene—one of them was an ancient wizard who had studied with Freud. The wizard recommended Rhineland Manor. He had a practice there. "It was his neck of the woods."

"And we never visited Irene?"

"Oh, you went once—but you had a crying fit. Mortimer had to drive you home."

"And she fell out of our lives."

Marla was more confused than ever. *She* had driven out Irene, she was the culprit, even if her skull had been on fire.

"Mummy, and you never missed her?"

"Miss her? She tore up my insides, rooted in me with that bullet of a head. I was just as bloody, even after she left the womb. We would have croaked. That's how much your father loved her."

3.

Marla grew more and more morose. Counselors and tutors looked after her girls. Roland Bourne was about to retire. Marla was the new motor of the firm. Once or twice a week she slept on the futon in her office. The tradition of Sunday brunches died, just like that. Marla's Indians, Hector and Paul, looked after Irene, when they didn't have to dig up dirt for Bregman, Bourne & Silk. There wasn't another pair of shadow men remotely like them. The DA's prize witnesses—angelic women without a blemish—became whores under their scrutiny. No one was safe on the stand. Manhattan politicians tempted Marla with a judge's robe. But she had little desire to sit behind a bench like some fanciful hawk. She would have lost the real aroma of the courtroom.

Marla seethed. Hostility was like a perfume—her Chanel N° 19. She shopped at Saks and was *unbreakable* in her Louboutins, her herringbone blazer, pin-striped pants, and blood-red scarf-tie. But where did all the anger come from? Was it the brittleness of her life? A dead father, absent daughters, an ex-husband who seemed to have disappeared, a sister with whom she had so little in common, and a mother who'd been crowned at college?

She had a short affair with her shrink. Marla was angrier than ever. She kept having problems with her paralegals. Either they were lazy and corrupt or they kept hitting on her partners at Bregman, Bourne & Silk. And the ones who were devoted to Marla would leave the firm once they found a husband. She couldn't survive in court without some paralegal to conjure up all of her notes and files on a computer screen, like a girl with a magic wand.

So Marla had to shop. She scoured the best agencies. And one afternoon a paralegal appeared at Marla's desk wearing Louboutins, a blood-red scarf-tie, and Chanel N° 19. The girl looked *curiously* familiar. Marla had never seen Little Sister in an Armani suit.

"Irene," she growled, "what the hell are you doing here?"

"The agency sent me, Sis."

"What agency?"

"Falconer, the one you always use."

The agency had tricked Marla, sending her own little sister without a note of warning. "Did you give them your real name?"

"Yes, Irene Silk of Central Park West."

It was like some fable out of a picture book, where the strangest things were suddenly familiar. Marla didn't believe a word.

"And how the hell did you become a paralegal? You didn't even have a high school diploma."

"I have one now," Little Sister said. "My little nieces helped me on their Macs. And I took courses online to help me with my paralegal studies."

"Who paid for it? I never received the bill."

"Oh," Irene said, purring in her pin-striped pants, "Mummy and the girls chipped in."

"And no one bothered to tell me?" Marla said, wallowing in her best courtroom manner. She could have been that *invisible* actress, Gracie Chance.

"It was meant to be a big surprise," Irene said, showing off her pointy red shoes.

"Well, Sis, will you hire me?"

Marla didn't have much of a choice.

"You'll have a two-week trial period, like every other paralegal I've considered."

That would be the end of it. Little Sister could never survive all the traps and snares. It was like stumbling around in a dark forest. Marla would give Irene a tiny bonus and send her away. Her paralegals had to juggle thirty, forty tasks, anticipate Marla's moves with no more than the blink of an eye. They had to assist Marla in the courtroom, hover around, visible and invisible at the same time.

Little Sister must have trained at a magician's college. She conjured up whatever legal precedent Marla required for a particular case, prepared her briefs, often knew more about her clients than Marla did, and how to soften a hostile witness for the kill. Prosecutors began to fear the paralegal in the pointy red shoes. And there was an odd metamorphosis. All that rough masculinity of a recluse fled from her face. She wore lipstick, polished her nails; she had the feline quality of a silver fox. She wasn't allowed to utter a word in open court, but judges watched her whisper in Marla's ear. And a minute later, Marla went for the throat.

"Ah, Mrs. Singleton, didn't you say in your last deposition that you'd *never* met the accused before the eleventh of March? And now, suddenly, you talk of 'a casual Christmas dinner' at Cipriani's and 'chance encounters' at the King Cole Bar well before March. I wonder how much *chance* there was in these encounters?"

It irked Marla, because the King Cole had once been her favorite haunt; it was where she prowled for men like a hunter in chalk stripes. And she didn't like the prosecution's star witness prowling where she herself had prowled. Marla's client was a billionaire who couldn't keep out of a trouble—Marcellus Bloom. A chemist and pharmaceutical king with a wife and five devoted children in Westchester, he would black out in Manhattan hotel rooms after slapping some woman he had hired to be slapped—there was never any sexual abuse, just a curious, contained violence. And vultures took advantage of his *addiction*, vultures like Mrs. Singleton. She had high-society status, hung around with politicians and art patrons, but was a con artist who soaked billionaires.

One of her predators lured Marcellus into a hotel room, let him perform his little tricks—he slapped Mrs. Singleton's accomplice a couple of times before he fell into his usual coma—and he woke up with an army of detectives and dusters in his room. Singleton herself had called the cops. Suddenly the *victim* had a whole catalogue of bruises. Marcellus was led out of the hotel in handcuffs. The *Daily News* called him Dr. Jekyll. The district attorney's men were like a band of lost children.

This was going to be their biggest case of the year—Marcellus Bloom caught battering a high-society housewife while Singleton worked behind the scenes like a puppeteer. She needed the *terror* of criminal court to shake some money out of Marcellus. But Marla's shadow men had dug a little deeper than the district attorney. And Irene had all the bits and pieces of the scam on her computer screen.

Marla broke Mrs. Singleton after five or six questions, revealed her whole extortion racket and her little stable of high-society housewives. The prosecutors were stunned as they watched all their hard work melt away. The judge was furious.

"I'd like to see counsel at sidebar."

Marla approached the bench with the prosecution team.

"I had a hunch, Your Honor. And it paid off."

The judge was still furious. His nostrils seemed to suck up all the air around him.

"Jurors will retire to the jury room. Bailiff, escort them out."

The district attorney's men didn't even put up a fight. The courtroom was cleared. Marcellus was staring at Irene.

"Marla, couldn't we have a drink with Little Miss Red Shoes?"

"Marcellus, if you ever go near my paralegal, you'll return to Westchester without your nuts."

4.

He was fifty years old, with the haunted handsomeness of Steve McQueen. He wasn't interested in starlets and gorgeous lady chemists. He went after waifs. He would seduce them with lines from Emily Dickinson about a wounded deer and voyages into eternity. And then he would pounce. There was nothing flamboyant about his moves: a single flower, dinner at a quiet bistro, and then a slight flutter in one eye as Dr. Jekyll turned into Mr. Hyde. It would have been comical, the tryst in a hotel room, the flower dug into the waif's hair, until he started slapping her around. But Marla's Indians had always been there for damage control. Hector and Paul would wash the girl's face, give her ten thousand in cash, send her home in a cab, wake Marcellus out of his torpor, and drive the billionaire to his Westchester estate.

These shadow men had their own rage. They would have loved to cripple Bloom.

"Get rid of him, Marla. He's bad news."

"But he keeps us in candy," she said. Yet she was startled by her own wanton ways. Hector and Paul had kept a "rogues' gallery" of slapped girls on their smartphones. These waifs were all wounded deer with frightened eyes. And now Mr. Hyde wanted to add Irene to his list. He pursued Little Sister with swatches of poetry tucked away in her e-mail like Valentine missiles. Marla had to sit down with Marcellus under the King Cole's rich brown light.

"You son of a bitch, she's my sister. I don't want her beaten up."

"You can't stop me from seeing Irene. She isn't in kindergarten."

"Oh, yes, she is," Marla said, scooping up a fistful of burnt almonds from the bar and tossing them into her client's face. She rushed back to Central Park West in a Lincoln Town Car. Irene stood in the foyer, putting on her eyeliner in one of Daddy's hammered-gold mirrors; the mirror was worth more than a little fleet of Town Cars. Lollie stood beside Little Sister, knotting her silk scarf.

"It's obscene," Marla said. "Mother, I thought you can't bear the sight of Little Sister."

There was such a look of contempt in Lollie's eyes, and meanness, that Marla nearly stumbled and had to step back.

"You haven't noticed a thing, have you?" Lollie asked, with the hauteur and pride of a homecoming queen. "I've grown fond of

Little Sister—in your absence, dear. You're at that sinister law firm seven days a week."

"That sinister law firm pays for your upkeep, Mummy."

"While you rescue stranglers," Lollie said.

"And Marcellus Bloom is one of those stranglers. So why are you encouraging Irene to go out with him?"

"He's not a strangler," Lollie said. "He sent me flowers. And he looks like Steve McQueen."

Now Irene stepped away from the mirror, like another homecoming queen. She wore a red dress with her Louboutins. Her arms were sleek and shiny. She could have been a red pearl.

"You're jealous, Sis, jealous that Marcellus wants me—you've always been jealous."

"But you've seen his file," Marla said, in a voice that was little more than a whisper. "He preys on women."

"Yeah," Irene said, "and let's hope he preys on me."

And Little Sister sailed out the door. Marla couldn't reach Hector and Paul. Neither of her Indians had a landline, and when she dialed their cells, she heard a loud whistle that nearly shattered her eardrums. She considered calling the cops—or the district attorney's office. But she couldn't blab on and on about a crime that hadn't been committed. They would laugh at her. So she had to wait, wait, wait . . .

Irene returned a little before midnight. There wasn't a mark on her face, but her eyeliner was smeared. She'd been sobbing.

"If he touched you," Marla said, "I'll . . ."

"You'll do what, Sis? Sue his ass. That will be some case. Will you put me on the stand, *counselor*?"

"What happened?"

"Nothing. That's the problem. We had some munchies at the King Cole. He kissed my hand. He wants to meet us both."

Jekyll and Hyde, Marla muttered to herself.

5.

It was the little ravaged land that Marcellus preferred for his escapades, a line of anonymous motels along Eleventh Avenue, where drag queens often met their rich clients; the area was cluttered with stretch limousines and abandoned bikes. The two sisters arrived by cab. The cabbie fled that desolation as fast as he could, even after Marla tipped him twenty dollars. Her hand was shaking. They entered the Sunshine Inn.

Hyde's Headquarters. They'd come to a bunker at the end of the world, with a neon sign, a littered courtyard, and mean little slits of glass in the front wall. She should have brought her shadow men, but she couldn't find them. The sisters were all alone.

"Can you believe this dump?" Irene asked.

The lobby had a single chair with a plastic cover, and the motel manager sat behind a metal grille. All that metal pocked his face, and he looked like some satanic creature sitting in the shadows.

Irene mentioned the billionaire, and Satan smiled.

"Ah, Mr. Marcellus. He's expecting you."

His eyes washed over the two sisters with obscene expectations.

"That guy has all the luck . . . hookers with red shoes."

Marla raged at him. "Shut your mouth." She dug into her purse and removed a card that her shadow men had given her from some detectives' fraternal order. Marla held the card close to the metal grille. "I can have your brains served to you on a silver platter."

"Sorry," the manager said. "I didn't . . ."

He buzzed them through a metal-plated door. Irene began to giggle.

"Sis, you scared the pants off him."

But Marla began to brood in the hall. The carpets were

mustard-colored, and the walls had sinister chalk stripes that seemed to mock her Armani pantsuit. *She* was the criminal, not Marcellus Bloom. Marla had created the monster, allowed him to flourish. He should have been locked away a long time ago, with Marla in the next cell.

She knocked on the monster's door and entered with Irene. He'd turned his lair at the Sunshine Inn into a fortress with bars on the windows. He wore a velour robe. It was his baby-blue eyes that made it so hard to convict him, not Marla's maneuverings. She was his accomplice, his *accessory.*

"My lovely girls," he said. "My lovely girls. Counselor, where were you keeping your kid sister all this time?"

"In my pocket," she said.

"That's not right. You have to share Irene."

His blue eyes had a sudden blaze. Soon he would be half out of his mind. But he still had his boyish grin, even while a vein pulsed above those blue eyes.

"Counselor, I want you to let me borrow Irene."

Marla didn't lash out at him. She was cautious now.

"But you could have stolen her—without my permission."

His eyes went mean. His nose twitched.

"That's no good," he said. "You have to give her away."

"Like a bride," Irene murmured, her face in the shadows. But Marla could feel a strange musk come from Irene—fire, sweat, and Chanel Nº 19.

"Yeah, like a bride," Marcellus said, grinning again. He glided about like a ballet dancer, tapped Marla once, twice on the cheek. The second tap was much harder than the first. "Marla dear, this place is locked down. It's a little complicated to get out."

"But, Marcellus," Irene said, "I don't want to get out."

He laughed with a stuttering growl. "That's what I like about you, kiddo. Marla has the brains, but you have all the juice. I recognized that right away."

Irene came out of the shadows. Marla could barely recognize her own sister. Irene had bloomed in the dark, like some exotic bulb with its own powerful heat.

"Let's get rid of her," she said. "Sis will only be in the way."

Marla shivered as Irene swallowed up the room with her musk.

"Sweetheart," Marcellus said, "I can't get rid of the counselor. She keeps me out of jail. But I love the idea."

And while Marcellus laughed, Irene took off one of her red shoes and pounded him on the head with its pointy heel. Marcellus' eyes fluttered. She pounded him again, like some celestial shoemaker.

Marla stood there, in some kind of coma. Irene grabbed her hand. "Sis, let's get the hell out of here."

She dragged Marla out of the room. They left tracks on the mustard-colored carpet. Marla heard a buzzer sound; the metal-plated door clicked open. Hector and Paul were waiting in the lobby. They'd torn a hole in the manager's metal grille. His head poked through the grille like an obscene toy. One of his eyes wandered. He could have been a dead man with a wandering eye.

"Marla," said one of the shadow men, "we let you down. Marcellus sent some Homeland Security agents after us, and we were out of commission for a little while."

"Damn it," Marla said. "Are you both illegals? I'll have to pay a heck of a fine."

"Shhh," they said, "it's all been rectified. And we'll straighten out this mess."

They sent the sisters home in a cab. Irene kicked off her red shoes. The cab arrived on Central Park West. The doorman saluted

Marla. She and Irene rode upstairs in an elevator car with some earth goddess hammered in silver into the rear wall; the goddess was surrounded by silver grapes. The building had gone up in the '20s, made of burnished red stone; it had once been a haven for silent film stars. One of the stars had leapt off the lip of her penthouse after the talkies ruined her career.

Lollie was waiting inside the door; she looked deranged. Her nightgown was hiked up, and Marla could spot her mother's purple kneecaps.

"Where have you been? I was worried half to death."

"Mummy, we were with Steve McQueen."

"You shouldn't make fun of me. I'm an old lady."

Lollie began to whimper. The two sisters walked their mother to her bedroom. The reservoir shone in the dark like a big fat jewel and blanketed the bedroom in a green glow. That eerie color clung to the crevices of Irene's face, turned it into a lantern. Marla bathed in all the wonder. Irene fluffed out Lollie's pillows with her fist. Then she slid Lollie under the covers and tucked her in.

"You won't leave me," Lollie whimpered. "You'll wait until I fall asleep."

She was like a wounded animal with purple kneecaps. Marla caressed her mother's knees.

"I lied," Lollie said. "Irene wasn't seventeen pounds. She was a gorgeous baby—too gorgeous. She never, never cried. . . . Irene, your father kept rocking you in his arms. You were his wolf cub."

Marla had a fit. "She wasn't a wolf cub, she wasn't. . . . Irene was a little girl."

"Yes," Lollie whimpered. "I shouldn't have lied . . . but don't leave me."

Marla wanted to run, wanted to flee Manhattan and all the little traps of criminal justice.

"We'll move to Seattle," she said. "Marcellus will never find us there."

But Irene held her in the grip of that green glow.

"And what should we do, Sis? Work for Wikipedia? I slaved my ass off to become a paralegal. We're irresistible in court."

With our red shoes, Marla muttered to herself

"I'm confused," Lollie said. "What's in Seattle?"

"Nothing, Mummy," Marla said. "Lattes and a lot of hills."

She could still see Little Sister pound Marcellus with the heel of her red shoe—the blows kept landing again and again, but it felt as if Marla's skull were on fire. And that fire would always be there, no matter where she went or what she did.

DEE

Dee remembered her first trip to the Bronx. She must have been six or seven. Daddy's driver, Somerset, drove them up from Manhattan in the limousine. She kept looking out the windows, and she realized now that she'd always been clicking, clicking with her eyes long before she had a camera and a light meter. Daddy was the director of Russeks Fifth Avenue, where the nabobs of Manhattan bought mink coats for their mistresses. Daddy was also a trustee at the Hospital and Home of the Daughters of Jacob. The home was on a hill in the Bronx, and it looked like a beleaguered castle with dull red walls and fire escapes that wavered in the wind.

The castle was filled with demented people in nightgowns, and Dee was riveted to them; she was as mischievous as any camera, as she devoured these shuffling old men and women with every bit of her being. The men had white unkempt hair, the women long braids knotted with rubber bands. Some of the women kissed her father's hand, flirted with him, addressed him in a language that was like a love song. Daddy was their savior. He sent them scraps of mink from Russeks that they wore as turbans in this hospital and home. He had brand-new radiators delivered to their rooms. But Dee wasn't at all interested in her father's philanthropy. She wanted to live here, amid the peeling walls, the constant sting of urine, the flatulence, and the overripe sweetness of decaying flesh.

Somerset had to pull her screaming out of the hospital's halls. The sickly faces had frightened her, yet she dreamt of touching the wild patches of hair that belonged to these old men. There wasn't one face as bewildering or as beautiful along Central Park West, where she lived in a monstrous cave of fourteen rooms at the San Remo.

Many years later, she saw that bewildering look in her father's eyes. It was the spring of '63, and Daddy lay dying of lung cancer. He had his own room at Mount Sinai. He was wearing silk pajamas, but he had the same sunken cheeks and wild patches of hair as the deranged old men at the nursing home in the Bronx. The silk pajamas couldn't save him. He went through some elaborate pantomime of pretending to write with a pen. He must have imagined he was still president of Russeks Fifth Avenue. She'd brought her paraphernalia to the hospital, had her cameras lashed to her neck. And she click-clicked the way she had done as a child in the Bronx, with the shutters of her own green eyes . . .

And now she was back in the Bronx, visiting with Eddie Carmel, a Jewish giant who was eight feet tall. Eddie longed to join a carnival, but he was much too ill. He suffered from scoliosis, and the Jewish giant had begun to shrink. He couldn't walk without a cane. And Dee was compelled by the sadness in his eyes. Dee was Eddie's accomplice. As a child she too had dreamt of running away to a circus or a carnival. She had felt like a freak on Central Park West, in that cave filled with furniture and cigarette smoke.

Even if he hadn't been ill, Eddie was much too smart to spend his days rotting in a carnival. He'd studied business administration at Baruch. Whenever Dee offered him a hint of one or two words, Eddie would construct a poem in his head.

"Deeyann," he'd say, "I dare ya."

And Dee would tempt him with some brain teaser. "No, I

dare you, Mr. Eddie Carmel. I demand a poem on the spot with a cement mixer and a flowerpot."

He'd laugh with that deep-throated laugh of his and recite in a voice that could have boomed back and forth between Manhattan and the Bronx.

Happy the flower, happy the pot
That can avoid all the mad fury
Of that fiend, the mixer of cement.

Eddie Carmel was born in Tel Aviv in 1936. He came from a family of rabbis.

His parents arrived in America when he was a little kid and settled in the Bronx. He wasn't much taller than any of his friends and classmates until he was a sophomore at Taft High School. He'd developed acromegaly, that curse of giants. But no one should have been surprised. His maternal grandfather had once been billed as the tallest rabbi in the world. By the time Ed was a senior, he couldn't sit in a classroom without occupying two chairs. At Baruch he took over the entire front of the class, and his instructors were trapped behind their desks. He couldn't even fit into his custom-made clothes. He grew all the time, like a merciless tree. And when he arrived at eight feet, he began to sprout in other directions; his jaw and forehead widened, his knuckles and his knees were like strange carbuncles.

She'd first met him around '58, when Eddie still dreamt of a normal life. He was selling mutual funds at an office close to Times Square. Normal life for Eddie included a desk that looked as long as an ocean liner; and he had to keep his great, lumbering shoes on a little table, because they couldn't fit behind the desk. Times Square had already become the mecca of freaks and misfits, with its penny arcades, its all-night movie houses, and Hubert's Dime Museum—that's where Dee had expected to stumble upon Ed, among sword swallowers and bearded ladies. But he wore a necktie behind his mammoth desk, a pitchman for mutual funds.

She crept all around him with her camera, while he sang to her like some local bard. He was the Jewish giant who protected kids in a neighborhood that could no longer protect itself. Gangs from the South Bronx would seize upon this tiny middle-class oasis, and there was Eddie, loping up and down the hills in his lumbering shoes, both David and Goliath.

But no matter how many times she clicked, she couldn't bring Ed out from under his mask of normalcy. He saw himself as some new-fangled squire. But he wasn't a squire. Customers came to him because of his outsize, not the advice he could give. And they stopped coming once his novelty began to wear off.

That's when she discovered him at the dime museum. Eddie Carmel had begun to moonlight as the World's Biggest Cowboy. He donned a Stetson and sat on some discarded king's throne. But she couldn't provoke Eddie with her camera, couldn't take him through the looking glass into some wonderland of his own. She caught nothing but his boredom and his big knuckles, even when she filmed him in the Bronx with his parents, who didn't seem to know what to make of their son.

He grew sick of moonlighting at dime museums and decided to conquer show business. He formed his own rock 'n' roll band, Frankenstein and the Brain Surgeons, even did a single, "The Happy Monster's Song," and then he had a few bit parts in films. But he couldn't keep playing Frankenstein with a clubfoot and enormous, clopping shoes. He sank into a circus. He was in the sideshow at Ringling Bros., but you couldn't find him on the circus' main floor, among the lions, the clowns, and the trapeze artists; Eddie's home at Madison Square Garden was underground.

You had to breathe sawdust and sweat in that fetid basement. And it had the same sting of urine as the Hospital and Home of the Daughters of Jacob. That's why Dee was drawn to this damp, dark world. But the home never had such a vast sea of faces. She clicked and clicked, with bolts of light that hurt people's eyes. Dee didn't really care. She was no longer a spy who hid from her own subjects. She was like a soldier on the attack. She relied more and more on her Mamiyaflex with an electronic flash that startled her subjects and would give them a haunted look. She was searching for shadows and ghosts, and for the shadow of herself.

But when she saw the Jewish giant on his platform, in a cartoonish cape, she couldn't bear to look into the deep sockets of his eyes. He was billed as the Tallest Man in America, but his back had already begun to curl. And he seemed about to totter. Children taunted the Jewish giant and stuck pins into his legs. And so Dee turned her electronic flash on them and attacked. The children scattered. But she didn't have the heart to seduce this battered Samson, to suck him into the whirlpool of her camera. She couldn't play Delilah with Eddie Carmel.

"Deeyann," he said, "if I stay here I'm gonna die."

Yet he did stay; the Jewish giant had nowhere else to go. He rarely traveled with Ringling Bros. He stood on his platform in the basement whenever the circus was in town. But he still lived at home with his parents in the Bronx. Eddie had learned to drive a Volkswagen by ripping out the front seat and sitting in the back. It was like his toy car. But his joints had grown too stiff for him to drive; he had to give up the Volkswagen. He loved the penny arcades, and sometimes he would wander with Dee through Times Square in his cowboy hat. And then he began inviting her home again. Dee felt like she was going on a date with the Jewish giant.

His parents were puzzled by this tiny woman who looked like

Peter Pan in her cropped hair. They hadn't seen her in seven years. Her eyes were almost sunk as deep as her son's. Dee never felt comfortable in that cramped apartment. The tiny living room was cluttered with cloth; each chair had a cloth cover; the couch had a cloth of its own. The lampshades had plastic covers; there were sconces in the wall that seemed to sprout light bulbs like sinister flowers. The windows were covered with drapes; the carpet on the floor reminded Dee of dead grass. The ceiling had veins in it that could have been the mark of some invisible leak.

Eddie's parents would leave them milk and cookies and retire to another room. The mother's name was Miriam. She wore a housecoat on Dee's visits. There was nothing in her face that revealed the simplest clue of Eddie's fate, even though it was her father who had been the tallest rabbi in the world. She seemed bewildered around him. Dee preferred Eddie's dad, who wore a mustache and was quite dapper in his velvet coat. But no matter how long Dee remained with Ed, moving like a pint-sized panther as he collapsed onto the couch, she couldn't capture the Jewish giant within her viewfinder; she was the haunted ghost, and Eddie was outside whatever a ghost could govern.

She had session after session with him in the Bronx; he was the same man-mountain, spectacular and absent, removed from her own mountain range. She was drawn to him, but Eddie Carmel had been her one great failure. She'd gone across the country in a Greyhound, had won her second Guggenheim, had her picture in *Time*, and had been dubbed the photographer of freaks. She went around in black leather skirts and white sweaters. She was in love with a married man. Marvin was her muse and her mentor—he made her giggle like a girl. She missed having her periods. She was forty-six years old. She had other lovers; sometimes they beat her up. Both of Dee's daughters were away. She lived alone. She'd visited hermaphrodites in Harlem, could feel her ghost mingle with theirs. Whenever she had to photograph some rich couple for *Harper's Bazaar*, she'd make them pose for six hours, until she broke through their boredom and unmasked the horror in their eyes.

And then she moved to Westbeth, an artists' complex in the West Village, near the Hudson River docks. It was a labyrinth of buildings that had once belonged to Bell Laboratories; Westbeth reminded Dee of a paupers' prison. Most of the artists who lived there were practically paupers. But Dee had a duplex with a heart-breaking view of the Hudson. Other artists and writers would have killed to live where she lived. Her own neighbors at Westbeth were jealous of her view. But there were parties all the time. Marriages broke up at Westbeth. Children cruised the dark, endless halls in tricycles and nearly ran her down. The elevators stank of cat piss. Westbeth began to feel like a penal colony, even with its theaters and dance troupes.

She was recovering from hepatitis; her skin looked gray. She could no longer eat processed food. She survived on raw honey and steamed vegetables. Marvin, her comrade and married lover, was away while she moved into Westbeth, and Dee was all alone. She couldn't prowl the halls like some vampire. So she prowled the streets with her cameras and her little kits. She'd once used a paper bag as a purse, but she had no need of purses now. She'd occupy some street corner, remain there for half the night, search every face, click with that crazy camera inside her head. Then she'd ride the Fifth Avenue bus down to the Village, hover near her fellow passengers, beleaguer them with her cameras, blind them for an instant with her flash, and sometimes the driver would toss her out of the bus and leave her stranded. But Dee didn't mind. She was the waif with cropped hair who lived in a paupers' castle.

And that's when Eddie Carmel called. She hadn't photographed him in two or three years. Dee couldn't become his own magic mirror and break into him with her camera. Ed was like a figure out of some fairy tale, and he lived within its walls with that trauma of his, the deep disgrace of his outlandish size. Ed was the aristocrat, not Dee. She'd been born a princess; Daddy had left her a disappearing treasure of mink coats and a dead department store. And now she was the princess of nothing at all.

Eddie had been forced to leave the circus in 1969. He could no longer mount the platform in the basement of Madison Square Garden. He wasn't even much of a giant; he'd shrunk below seven feet. And how could the Jewish Goliath protect his streets from marauders? He couldn't run after the Jesters and the Fat Cats of Clay Avenue.

"Be cautious, Deeyann, on your ride to the Bronx. If you run into some bad people, tell them you know Eddie Carmel."

But she ran into no one, into nothing but dust on the subway. She rode uptown on the D train, ceiling fans creaking over her head. She was always lost in the Bronx, no matter what line she took, no matter where she exited. She happened to be on a hill beside Daddy's hospital and home. She hadn't visited those demented women and men at the Daughters of Jacob in forty years. And it was remarkable how the walls of that dull red world reminded her of Westbeth. The corridors hadn't been so dark at the hospital and home, and the main traffic consisted of wheelchairs rather than tricycles. Dee remembered the baked apples on the radiator in some old couple's room, how she and Daddy had shared a baked apple the couple had offered them, how Daddy broke into the apple's flesh with a silver spoon he'd brought up to the Bronx. She grew dizzy from all that sweetness, as the apple bubbled on the radiator and filled half the hall with an intoxicating perfume. Daddy had been so kind to that couple. His own parents had come from Kiev, had eloped and run away to America. He seldom invited them to the San Remo, but perhaps he must have seen his father and mother in this old couple . . .

Dee began to cry. Was she mourning her father, or was it something else? She felt like Alice in a wonderland that was both familiar and remote. She marched deeper into the Bronx, strode across the Grand Concourse with her cameras and her bags. There was a little armada of beauty shops on the ground floors of apartment houses that could have belonged to some doll's version of Central Park West. She walked down a hill, crept under the shadows of the Jerome Avenue El, and climbed another hill. She landed on a little island called Kingsland Lane. And she could have walked out of a dream. There was the giant's house at the very edge of the island.

She climbed the stairs, which were like another hill. She was agitated when Eddie opened the door. He had stubble on his face. His hair seemed much curlier than it had ever been. His back had a noticeable bump on it. He was very frail and now had two canes. But he seemed concerned about Dee's condition, not his own.

"Deeyann," he said, with a quiver in that deep echo chamber of his. "What happened to you? You're a bundle of bones."

He was kind enough not to talk about her gray complexion. Dee's skin looked liked the paste she had used in kindergarten. Eddie's mother welcomed her with milk and cookies. And Dee was startled by the mother's own complexion. As Eddie unraveled, he resembled Miriam more and more. They had the same curly hair, the same big nose, the same freckles. Dee carried her own apple in a camera bag, but she drank the milk and munched on Miriam's cookie. Nothing had changed much in the flat. The furniture and the lamps were still sheathed in plastic and cloth. The veins had spread across the ceiling like some perverse hieroglyphic. The carpet was a little dirtier but still looked like dead grass.

His mother and father were about to withdraw, but Dee held them with her own invisible string, soothed them with little nonsense songs, like the patter of a mockingbird. Then she appealed to the giant.

"Ed, I'd like to try some photos with you and your mom and dad."

"They're shy," he said. "They're not like me. They've never been near a circus, Deeyann."

Perhaps he wasn't eager to share the landscape of the photograph with his mom and dad. And she wondered if she'd ever capture Eddie Carmel. She'd photographed Charles Atlas at his home in Palm Beach, had caught him among his trappings, the mile-long drapes, the chandeliers, the crystalline lamps, and there he was, a seventy-six-year-old muscleman who'd marketed himself and now looked like a tanned monster waiting for his death; she'd unmasked the quiet dignity of dwarfs in rooming houses; she'd photographed mothers with swollen bellies in the backwoods of South Carolina, captured the undaunted look of campers at a posh camp for overweight girls in the heart of Dutchess County; she'd revealed the mad, wrinkled fury of Mae West in her Santa Monica fortress, but she failed year after year with Eddie Carmel.

She smiled, she wheedled, she danced around Ed like a coquette, and finally the faltering giant agreed to pose with his parents. And she also had to wheedle them. They would rather have sat behind a closed door and not be reminded of the monstrosity in their living room. Dee couldn't have coaxed them without Eddie.

"Ah, come on, it's for posterity."

And then he revealed his wickedness in a gentle way. He tried to straighten his crooked back, preened for a moment, and said, "Deeyann, isn't it awful to have a midget mom and a midget dad?"

Mr. and Mrs. Carmel didn't laugh. They posed with their giant son. He had to lean on them; his parents had become Eddie's twin canes. They stared into her camera, but something was wrong in this family portrait. Eddie Carmel was still the performer, still the star. His big ears overwhelmed the frame. Dee clicked and clicked—nothing happened. She was forlorn. Then he fumbled with his canes and stood without the help of his mom and dad. She caught him in profile, with one of his canes hidden and much of his vanity gone. Mr. and Mrs. Carmel looked up at Ed like immigrants who had spawned a monster in the New World, and Eddie clutched his canes and stared back at his mom with an aloof tenderness that only a giant could have. Dee clicked. Eddie stood there in his wrinkled pants while Mrs. Carmel was in a daze and Mr. Carmel struck his own pose, with a hand in his pocket, distancing himself from all giants and his son . . .

One of the art directors she'd worked with had called her a huntress, and she probably was. She'd found what she wanted—it was as if the image itself had pressed the shutter. Some of her compassion had fled after that click. She wouldn't photograph Eddie Carmel again, and now she was trying to distance herself, the way Eddie's dad had done. But she couldn't. Eddie Carmel clung to her bones.

By some miracle she scrambled down from Eddie's hill with all her paraphernalia and was able to find the subway. But her elation didn't last. Once she arrived at her pauper's castle near the docks, she fell into a crippling gloom. She began to phone people at random. While she chatted with some curator at an art museum in Kansas, Dee pretended she was a mermaid following a barge on the Hudson, but even that couldn't console her. She smoked a little pot. All the belief in her own power was gone—the right to stir up some mischief in a portrait session, and then to hold that mischief in the frame. She felt guilty about the giant. She'd stolen into his life, posed him and his family like a minor-league Velázquez, while she stood there, a lurking presence in the photograph. She'd manipulated Eddie Carmel. She was better off posing Mae West. Dee didn't mind stealing from her. Mae West was a profusion of masks. Dee had caught the rage under her creams and cocoa butter—the madness of decrepitude.

But Eddie Carmel was visited by old age before he was old, and even that couldn't anger him. She shouldn't have pursued the giant. Distressed, she began to doze in the dark. She forgot to unplug the phone. She fumbled for it as the ringer ripped into her sleep.

"Deeyann, it's me."

Eddie Carmel listened to her cry. "I'm a tramp," she said. "I'm a stinking siren. I took advantage of you, Ed. I'll tear up all the rolls of film."

"Calm down. Mom said she's glad I have a friend like you."

"I'm a witch."

"Ah, but I'm blue without ya, Dee. I can't dream up a poem . . . give me a hint, huh?"

But she had no hints. Her mind was all scrambled. Eddie pleaded with her.

"Have a heart."

And she came out of her gloom. She scratched her chin with her own normal-sized knuckles, while she recalled the carbuncles on Eddie's hands.

"Hill," she said. "Hill . . . and court jester."

"Ah, that's a real conundrum," he said, as he started to compose.

Look at the giant who lives on the hill
He laughs and he cries like a court jester
But one morning he swallowed the wrong pill
And now the whole world can watch him fester.

Eddie Carmel roared at his creation; his poem was as sad as the dwarfs Dee filmed in their rooming houses, but the giant's deep, rippling laugh went right through the wires.

"Dee, I'm helpless. I can't write a poem without you."

He hung up, but the echo of that roar remained in her ears.

PRINCESS HANNAH

Harrington fell.

It wasn't cocaine. It wasn't alcohol. It was circumstance. His wife left him, took his kids away. Her name was Charlotte, and she had a college degree. Harrington had never gone to college. He could barely write a paragraph, and Charlotte was a great reader of books. That's what had attracted him to her: Charlotte was a witch with words. Harrington had his own silent poetry—the deep sadness in his face—but that wasn't enough. They were lovebirds for a little while. She bore Harrington two boys. But the boys soon turned against him. They must have recognized Charlotte's disenchantment with Harrington; they'd watched him beat her up. She ran to another city. He could have tracked her down, but he didn't have the resources. He always existed at the edge of things.

He was a packer at a chocolate factory, earned decent money, but he was paid off the books. The factory loved to hire "ghosts" like Harrington. His wife had worked as a kindergarten teacher, covered the children and Harrington on her health plan, so he could drift, and now he had to drift alone.

He'd been sleeping with the boss's wife, Diane, who also worked at the factory. He would improvise, catch her in a closet. It was furtive and quick, but Diane must have squealed on him. Perhaps she was also sleeping with another man and had used

Harrington as a scapegoat. The boss had a tribe of brothers and sisters, and this tribe slapped Harrington across the factory in front of all the employees.

He had welts on his face for weeks. He couldn't find a job. He had no references. He washed dishes for a while, but he would get into fights. Harrington lost his apartment. He moved in with an old high school buddy of his, Martin Hare, known as "the Scooter," because he was always scurrying around. Both of them were forty-one and had dreams of making a fortune, but neither knew where to begin. They weren't gangsters or commercial pirates. Harrington was still handsome, in spite of the welts. Scooter was a gnome.

"We'll be rich," the Scooter would say. "You'll see."

They decided to rob the chocolate factory, so that Harrington could have his revenge on Stillwell, his boss. It was the Scooter's idea.

"It wouldn't work," Harrington said. "I've never used a gun."

"Come on," the Scooter said. "I know a toy shop. They have guns that look realer than the real thing."

"Like what?"

"The Colt Commander, Beretta Jetfire . . ."

Harrington couldn't understand a word, but he went to the toy shop, and Scooter was right. The guns in the window could frighten a hundred chocolate factories. Harrington bought plastic Colt Commanders for the Scooter and himself. Tuesday afternoon was the ripest time for a robbery. Stillwell would take out all the cash he collected from the factory's little retail shop and bring it to the bank. Harrington and the Scooter would wait for him in Halloween masks that Scooter had kept from childhood. The masks were a little too tight. But they didn't really mind. They rehearsed the robbery, mapped out their positions as if they were preparing some kind of imbecile ballet.

They stood at the side door in their masks, and when Stillwell appeared, both of them waved their tin guns and demanded Stillwell's cashbox. But they didn't see the pistol in the boss's pants. Stillwell shot the Scooter. Harrington struggled with him, managed to get the pistol away and bring the Scooter back home, but in his panic he'd forgotten all about the cashbox.

"Partner," the Scooter whispered, "we did good, didn't we?" And he died in Harrington's arms.

Harrington couldn't afford to bury him, and how could he comfort a dead man with a bullet in his side? He left the Scooter in his favorite chair, locked the door, and decided to live on the lam.

Somebody grabbed Harrington's tin gun on his first night out, kicked him in the head while he was sleeping near the ventilation duct of a midtown office building. "Hey, motherfucker," a voice crooned at him in the dark, "that's my mattress." There was no mattress. There was a tiny heated space, in the wild of winter. His chin was bleeding, and he didn't even have the consolation of a toy gun. He wandered across the city. He had no more plans. He was like a blind laborer in a dream. Some cursed intuition must have guided him to the downtown processing center of the city's public shelters. It wasn't shut in the middle of the night, but he couldn't find one official to feed him, only a nurse with a Band-Aid.

Men with stranger eyes than his began to collect around six A.M. A woman with a slightly scarred face interviewed him. She was kind to Harrington. She let him have a doughnut and a cup of coffee. He couldn't tell her about the killing, talk about his job at the chocolate factory. He was like a stateless person. He'd lost his Social Security card, couldn't recall the number.

"How can I process you, Mr. Harrington?"

"My wife worked for the city. I was covered on her plan."

"Where is your wife?"

"Disappeared."

The woman must have pitied Harrington. She encouraged him to invent a Social Security number.

"Lie a little," she said. He was processed in half an hour. A bus brought Harrington and fifty other homeless men to an old armory on a hill above a housing project in the Bronx. He entered an enormous barrack and couldn't believe the smell. It was like living in an ocean of unwashed feet. There were hundreds of beds in the barrack, which probably had housed the National Guard—weekend soldiers who would train at the armory with toy guns like Harrington had used in his botched heist. But there weren't any weekend soldiers now. The barrack was overheated, and Harrington should have rejoiced. He was out of the cold. But the heat only multiplied the stench that rose up off the walls and made his nostrils quiver and his eyes burn.

The guards wouldn't leave him alone. They touched Harrington's pockets, searching for loot, told him he couldn't sleep in his bed during the afternoon unless he paid them a toll.

"Sunlight money," they said.

Harrington blinked. They tapped his knees with their billy clubs. "Hey, little fellah, you aren't supposed to occupy your bed until the sun goes down."

But the beds were packed with sleeping men, who blocked out the sunlight with their blankets, built their own tents with filthy sheets.

"Did they all pay their toll?" Harrington asked, pointing to the tents.

"Certainly," the guards said. And they tapped his knees a little harder. But they were helpless scavengers compared to the little band of men that ruled the shelter, calling themselves "the Constables," because several of them were ex-cops who'd spent time in jail. They all had other residences, but they operated out of the armory, where they could rob, sell drugs, and form their own prostitution ring. They bribed the guards, smuggled in women, and used transvestites at the shelter as their sexual slaves. The transvestites adored Jacob Faust, the Constables' chief. He was a one-eyed maniac who'd been with the military police. He had a Colt Commander tucked inside his pants, and it wasn't made of tin. He terrorized the whole shelter, demanded sexual favors, and when he first saw Harrington, he went insane.

"I'm in love," he announced to his gang. He walked up to Harrington, handed him a dress. "You'll wear this for me."

But Harrington was much too tired to be afraid; an anger had been welling in him. He pulled the Colt Commander out of Jacob's pants, aimed it at an invisible sky, and pulled the trigger. A chandelier fell from the ceiling like some bald, prehistoric bird. All its crystal was already gone. No one even remembered that the armory had a chandelier. And Harrington could have been a magical hunter who'd come into the Constables' lives.

"You wear the dress," he screamed at Jacob Faust.

"What?"

"Wear the dress."

Jacob Faust put the dress on over his shirt and pants. The Constables started to titter. Jacob walked out of the shelter and never returned. But Harrington couldn't take his place. The Constables wouldn't approach some crazy man who'd shot a chandelier. Harrington was outside whatever quilted community had formed at the shelter. He ate breakfast alone, and he couldn't afford to sleep. The Constables would have smothered him with pillows or stabbed him with their knives. He had to lie like a stone man in his bed at night, listen to every noise, clutch the Colt Commander in his fist. He would think of Charlotte and his children, of Scooter with blood leaking out the side of his belly, of that woman at the processing center with scars on her face. The scars had lent her a curious beauty . . . and a curious light. Why hadn't he asked the woman her name?

But he wouldn't have survived the shelter very long. He dozed once, dreamt of the woman—she was dancing at the center, taking off her clothes—and the Constables were upon him with their pillows. He had to shoot out one of the windows, or they wouldn't have gone back to bed.

Harrington had to laugh. He was always attracted to damaged goods. Crippled toads, women with scars on their faces. He stole out of the armory in the middle of the night with his Colt Commander. He had no cash. He crossed two bridges and reached the processing center as the sun was rising. But the woman wasn't there. . . . He asked the other officials about her.

"You know. The nice lady . . . with the scar."

"Ah, Princess Hannah. She doesn't work for Human Resources. She's only a volunteer. She comes and goes."

"But what's her real name?"

"Hannah. We started calling her the princess, because she's kind to all the crapheads . . ."

"Does she have a Social Security number?"

"Don't start getting personal."

"But where can I find her?

"In the streets, looking for scumbags to save."

Harrington searched the streets; he couldn't find Princess Hannah. He was only one more bum in an army of bums, and that army seemed to have expanded while Harrington had spent two nights in a public shelter. He belonged to a planet of homeless men. Still, Harrington had a Colt in his pants. He could sleep under a pile of newspapers, and if anybody disturbed him, he'd pull out his gun.

Harrington was always hungry. It didn't matter how many bottles he stole off the milk trucks. Milk was never enough. He scavenged, like other homeless men, learned about the little depots where bakers dumped their spoiled goods, but how many loaves of bread could he eat with rotten blue marks in the middle? He began using his Colt. At first he robbed homeless men who had a little more plunder than he did, and then he picked off people coming out of the subway on winter nights. They never seemed to have much cash on them, and he couldn't get rich during those raids; when one of the women swooned with Harrington's gun in her face, he felt guilty and fetched her a glass of water.

"Please, I won't harm you. I'm a homeless man."

The woman blinked at Harrington, who ran back into the winter haze without her wallet. But he had to do something about his hunger pains. His clothes started to rot. He couldn't enter a restaurant or sit in the library to keep out of the cold. He was too ashamed of his shabbiness. He smashed the window of a men's clothing shop in the midst of his fury. He didn't enter the shop. He reached into the window and plucked some clothes off the mannequins' backs. It was the first bit of fun he'd had in weeks. The mannequins didn't cry; none of them was burdened with a silly human heart.

He went around like a gigolo in spring colors and Italian shirts and shoes. The shoes didn't fit, and Harrington limped along, had bunions to deal with. But now he could go into the library, examine a couple of the books that Charlotte adored. He couldn't get beyond the first paragraph. His concentration was shot. He'd become a creature of the wilderness.

He ate lots of sandwiches and fat pizza pies. He continued with his holdups. But he wouldn't prey on women. Soon his Italian clothes were ragged and he was more of a werewolf than ever. He considered blowing his brains out.

And then he saw a figure in a snowstorm, a limping man dressed in the finest clothes, and the man was strangely familiar. Harrington had trouble with sentences, but he wouldn't forget a face. Ghosts were wandering around in that storm, and Scooter's ghost was among them.

Harrington nudged the ghost with his gun. "Gimme all you got." The ghost glared at him. "With a toy gun?"

Harrington shot a hole into the crown of the ghost's hat.

"You son of a bitch," the ghost said. "You left me there to die. Didn't even call an ambulance."

"But you were dead," Harrington muttered. "I listened to your heart."

"You a doctor all of a sudden? You a specialist? Where'd you get that gun?"

"I took it off a bad guy. . . . Scooter, is it me who's dead? Or did you dance out of the fucking snow?"

"Dance?" the ghost said. "I'm a cripple because of you . . . the neighbors found me, ran me over to the hospital. It was touch-and-go. I had to drink that liquid shit, the slop that drips into your veins. I lost my appetite, and I'll never get it back."

"But why are you limping?"

"I had a blood clot," the ghost said. "It turned into phlebitis."

"Did the cops ask you questions, Scooter?"

"I didn't snitch. I told 'em a robber came in through the window. They had to believe me. Who would invent such a story? I gave up my apartment. Fuck all the landlords. I'm living in a convalescent home. A lady looks after us."

"What kind of lady?"

"A lady," Scooter said. "But she's different. She suffered."

And Harrington felt a tingle rush down his spine, as if he had a serpent inside his clothes. "Does she wear a scar on her face?"

Scooter's eyes began to pop. "Harrington, how'd you guess?"

"And her name is Princess Hannah."

"Shh, it's a state secret. She handpicks us . . . the guys who convalesce. People take advantage of her. She has to raise her own money. The city don't give her shit."

"I'm going with you, Scooter . . . to Princess Hannah."

"That's impossible," Scooter said. "You're not a cripple. Hannah wouldn't let you in."

It was a battered little mansion at the edge of a park, and Harrington felt sorry for the princess, who ran a convalescent home that needed to convalesce. She greeted him at the door, and he was still troubled by the ferocious beauty of her scars.

"Told him not to come," the Scooter said, jumping up and down on the wooden stairs. "He's certifiable. He put a hole in my hat."

But Harrington wasn't listening to the Scooter. "Hannah," he asked, "do you remember me?"

She had pieces of hair over her pale blue eyes. "How could I forget the man without a Social Security number?"

She was Harrington's height, and her blond hair was streaked with silver. The scars seemed to camouflage her age. She could have been a year or two younger than Harrington, or a bit older. He could almost feel her ample body under the dress she wore.

"He can't stay," the Scooter said. "He ain't crippled. He ain't even sick. And he treats his friends like dirt."

Hannah smiled. "But he's standing at our door."

"He tricked me. I didn't mean to bring him."

"I could use a handyman," Hannah said. "But I can't pay you a dime . . . just room and board."

He couldn't take his eyes off Princess Hannah. The wound of his marriage was already gone.

He didn't have to sleep in the dormitory. He had a room of his own. It was barely bigger than a closet, but he could dream without hearing garbled groans. His room was next to Hannah's, and he'd go to bed imagining her body. He had to hide his erection at the dinner table. He'd follow her around, do whatever chore she demanded of him. Hannah wasn't licensed. She didn't even have a doctor in the house. She was nurse and cook and den mother to cripples she'd find in the street. The city could have closed her down. But it didn't care enough about the drifters in Hannah's domain. She was tolerated: Princess Hannah. And Harrington was crazy, crazy in love.

He'd stutter when he talked, but he wouldn't spy on her, peek into her room. The princess slept alone at night. She was a hermit like Harrington and the other refugees in the dormitory. She'd wander out of the mansion, wearing white gloves, and badger different philanthropists to fund her home. But they always refused her. Hannah would mimic them. " 'It's brave of you, dear. If only you had a license . . . and a genuine nurse.' "

Hannah's refugees would come up to her while she sat over her soup. "We'll sell raffle tickets, we'll get you some cash." They'd stroke her silver-and-blond hair, surround her soup plate. It was only Harrington who held back. He could imagine the relentless electricity if he ever touched her hair.

His door opened one night. He had a visitor. He tried to conjure up Hannah's perfume, but Harrington's visitor hardly had a scent. He still wished it was her. The visitor moved close in the dark, and Harrington's heart pumped and pumped until he caught the unmistakable whiff of laundry soap. "Scooter, what the fuck do you want?"

"Keep quiet. You'll wake the princess."

Harrington snapped on the light. Scooter's ears were glowing. He looked like a lantern. Harrington could have shot his eyes out and wouldn't have felt a thing.

"We have to take up a collection," Scooter whispered. "Have our own Salvation Army."

"How?"

"With your gun."

Harrington groaned. "Would you like a bullet on the other side of your belly?"

"Won't happen again. We were amateurs, with toy store stuff. Partner, nobody's gonna stop us with that Colt."

"Stop us, Scooter? Are you a general? It's not so easy to stick up a man. You have to look him in the eye."

"We'll look . . . can't you tell? The princess is desperate."

"She could give up the mansion, let us make our own little winter. Why's she so good to us?"

"It ain't goodness. It's stronger than that. Hannah was ruined."

"What you talking about? She could win a beauty contest."

"With that face . . . and that body?"

"What does a runt like you know about Hannah's body?"

"Nothing. But I know it was ruined . . . her husband scalded her."

"Hannah has a husband?"

"She's entitled," Scooter said. "She wasn't born in a convent. And her husband threw a big pot of boiling water at her. She was in the hospital for months . . . and then she lived out on the street, sucked on a bottle. No one took care of Hannah, so she built a home for people like herself."

"But why'd Hannah's husband do such a crazy thing?"

"He was jealous."

"Come on," Harrington said. "Jealousy doesn't get you to throw a pot of water at your wife."

"Sure it does. . . . That's the downside of love."

"And what's the upside?"

"Perfect passion."

"Some philosopher," Harrington said. "Did you ever have perfect passion?"

"Once or twice. What about you?"

"Never. I never had it."

"Then I pity you," the Scooter said and walked out of Harrington's room.

He couldn't eat, couldn't sleep. He had to deliver himself from his own acute ache. He didn't have the nerve or the talent to confront Hannah, declare his love. He tried his wife's way. With a note. It took him a week to scribble a few stinking lines.

> Dear Hannah,
> Your handyman loves you. Don't be alarmed.
> He wouldn't do something uninvited. But if my message bothers you, I will go.
> Harrington

He left the note in Hannah's mailbox. He'd return to the mailboxes every hour to see if Hannah had retrieved the note. Finally, on his sixth trip, he saw that she'd emptied her mailbox. He still couldn't sleep. And all the while he did his chores, Hannah never mentioned the note.

She kept searching for patrons. She wore her white gloves. She wasn't unkind to Harrington, didn't punish him for his scribbles. But he couldn't leave the slightest dent in Hannah's life.

He would pace in his room all night, and for one instant he saw outside his agony: Hannah's door was open. And Harrington followed the path of his own dreamless dream. He entered the Princess's room. She was lying under the covers, with Harrington's note in her fist. She didn't object when he crawled under her blanket. And she didn't attempt to hide her scars. They were like crooked silver lines. Hannah's scorched skin. She could have been made of phosphorous or beaten bits of silver and gold. And while he lay next to her, her heart cupped in his hand, he thought of the Scooter. Perfect passion. What's perfect passion compared to Princess Hannah?

She wasn't tender with Harrington outside the borders of her bed. He was the princess's handyman. He never sat with her at supper or tried to fondle Hannah while she was giving him instructions about his various chores. The refugees seemed to know about Harrington's nighttime excursions into the princess's room, but when they smiled at her, she wouldn't smile back. The princess was occupied with money matters. She couldn't pay the electric bill. Harrington disappeared for two hours and returned with a hundred dollars. He'd taken the Scooter's advice and had become a highwayman. He'd cover his face with a handkerchief and rob whoever he could: motorcyclists, truck drivers, delivery boys. . . . He even held up an entire bus, though he wouldn't interfere with grandpas and grandmas.

She didn't ask him where he got the money, didn't comment on the Colt inside his pants. But he couldn't seem to have a conversation with her. The words wouldn't come. And then he gathered up his courage, shut his eyes, and said, "Tell me about your husband, Hannah, please."

"There's nothing to tell. He was a son of a bitch."

"But if he hadn't scalded you, we might never have met."

"That's wonderful. Why don't you thank him, get in touch?"

"I didn't mean that. But Scooter said he was jealous, and—"

"Jealous of what? He stole from me. And when I caught him at it, he figured he would burn me alive."

"Hannah . . ."

"Stop talking, Harrington. Write me another letter."

"I can't. I'm poor with sentences."

"Not so poor," she said.

She brought him into her room. It wasn't even midnight. She undressed Harrington and then undressed herself. She was like a mermaid with silver on one side. He kissed every silver wound.

> Dear Hannah,
> I dream in rainbows.
> I trace all our scars in my sleep.
> I'm a selfish man, in love with loving you.
> I . . .

Harrington couldn't finish his letter. He had to play the highwayman. His princess couldn't settle with the butcher and her laundry service without his particular skills. But he was absent-minded, thinking of words, when he should have concentrated on his next victim, his next mark. He put on his handkerchief mask a bit sloppily, half his mouth showing, and attacked a Chevrolet parked outside a deserted storefront. If he hadn't been dreaming, he might have sniffed the plainclothesman inside the car.

"Friend," he said, like a pragmatic highwayman, "gimme your money, nice and slow."

The plainclothesman shot Harrington in the groin. Harrington slapped him on the head with his Colt. Then he limped away. It took him an hour to walk the ten blocks to Hannah's mansion. He was crying. She wouldn't be able to greet the butcher with cash in her hand.

. . . in love with loving you.

He got to the dormitory. He couldn't see a thing. Blood was in his eyes. The Scooter found him, screamed, "Mother of God." And Hannah rushed over from her desk, where she was wishing away all her liabilities, all her debts. She reached out, and Harrington tumbled into her arms. Ah, he felt secure against her damaged skin. He wasn't dreaming now. "Darling," she said, just before he died.

MILO'S LAST CHANCE

He stumbled from school to school, became an embarrassment, suffering from periodic fits of silence in front of his students. The sachems at the Education Department didn't know what to do with Mr. Cartwright. He was much too young to retire. They couldn't reward him with a disability pension. He wasn't disabled. He met with lawyers and administrators at the department's new headquarters in lower Manhattan. It was, they said, Milo's last chance.

He was sent to a barrio in the South Bronx where no teacher or student had ever prospered. He would finish out his days in "Siberia" or wouldn't finish at all. It was a special high school for the hardest cases, housed in an abandoned fire station near Boston Road. He was a misfit in a school for misfits. But he felt comfortable around a bunch of kids who had already been condemned to a life of non-learning—the Bronx's own prodigal daughters and sons from housing projects that were little better than high-rise caves.

Milo himself was a prodigal son. He'd graduated from Columbia at fifteen, had been awarded a fellowship to study English literature at Oxford. But he began talking to Shelley and Byron and Keats in the middle of Manhattan. His father, a reputable accountant, decided to put Milo into a teacher training program at Hunter College. Education classes wouldn't tax his mind. But he began to drift . . . until he arrived in the South Bronx.

This revamped fire station was paradise. Its students could have been tailored for Milo. They expected nothing from him, nothing at all, and he sang to them about the poets who were still inside his head—Lord Byron with his clubfoot or the consumptive Keats, who spat up blood while he scribbled. Milo didn't analyze poems in class. He told them a hundred tales, and his students were in ecstasy. Byron and Keats could have lived in their housing projects. They knew plenty of people who spat blood or staggered around with a clubfoot.

His dad had bought him a studio on Jane Street as a kind of "insurance policy." But Milo Cartwright felt estranged from this land of coffeehouses and pet hospitals and stores that sold nothing but cupcakes. He preferred the brick wilderness of the Bronx. He'd become an icon in the barrio, a secular saint—"Mr. C."—who taught poetry without ever reading a poem.

The sachems downtown didn't bother him. Milo was getting results. He would find a rare prodigy—a girl from Senegal or a boy from Martinique—who dared dream of college, and Milo tutored such prodigies, helped them write a decent composition. He encouraged students to start their own little library, bought them their first bookcase. He now had a makeshift office, a closet really, without a window or proper ventilation. He'd become the school's guidance counselor in addition to his other chores. This school for outcasts had never had a guidance counselor. It never needed one until Milo came along. Suddenly it had candidates to the best colleges.

He often ate lunch in his office. But one afternoon he drifted into the cafeteria, and there she was, wearing the same purple lipstick. He shivered at the sight of her. Her eyes burrowed into him like bullet holes.

"Are you so stuck-up, Mr. C., that you can't even acknowledge one of your old flames?"

"I never had a flame."

He'd been a student teacher at William Howard Taft nine or ten years ago. And she was a wildflower of the West Bronx—tall and voluptuous, she could dazzle you with her purple lipstick and big brown eyes. She was notorious in the neighborhood as the mistress of a married fireman. The principal had been looking to toss her out of Taft. But Tanya Greenblatt never misbehaved within the school's walls. And yet she flirted with Milo, who couldn't have been that much older than Tanya. He was drawn to the boldness of her brown eyes. But he never saw her outside of school. He didn't dare. He was an apprentice, a teacher on trial.

And once, while Milo was monitoring exams, he caught her copying from another student. He didn't want to hurt Tanya Greenblatt, but his own attraction had demonized him, and he found a way to claw at the girl. He should have warned her first, but he sent her to the principal. She was thrown out of school.

And here she was, working as a scullion in a cafeteria. Several of her teeth were missing. She had a gray streak on her left eyebrow, as if some bad angel had visited Tanya and left its mark. She was still in her twenties and looked like some ruined Cleopatra. But it terrified Milo to be near her. He was still drawn to Taft's wilted wildflower.

"I'm sorry," he said. "I shouldn't have reported you to the principal."

Her face softened. And she was almost beautiful again, even with the gaps in her mouth. He couldn't reveal how much he had liked her, not in the middle of the cafeteria, with students and teachers spying on him. She'd been working at this renegade school a whole year, had seen Milo in the halls many times, and didn't want to trouble him with her own troubles—at least that's what Milo imagined.

And then she disappeared, wandered out of the cafeteria and never came back. He might have gotten her address from the school clerk. But he wouldn't bother a gap-toothed goddess who wanted to be alone. And he suffered. He'd had few friends. Locked into himself, he lacked the simplest powers of seduction. He could commune with the dead, debate with Byron and Keats, and talk about them to kids who had such a hard time reading a book. He struggled with his students until they began to sing out words like some wild soprano. The principal, Dr. Muldoon, was in awe of Milo. Letters from Harvard and Yale shot across his desk like missiles from another land. Dr. Muldoon was enjoying his new fame.

But Milo was miserable, haunted as he was by Tanya and her missing teeth. He'd drift through the cafeteria, hoping he could conjure her up with the squeeze of an eye—his own feeble magic failed him. And while muttering to himself in a composition class, his coat covered in chalk as he tried to explain the difficulty of gerunds, he found Tanya Greenblatt in the front row. Had she arrived on the wings of her own bad angel? She had a notebook now, and she clung to his words as he scratched a sentence on the board in his own strange scrawl.

The young lady arrived without our noticing who she was.

His students couldn't find the hidden observer, couched right in front of the gerund.

"*Our,*" he said. "That lone word sneaks in like a snake and corrupts the sentence."

"Then pluck it out, Mr. C.," said Marguerita of Boston Road.

"And what would happen? The young lady in the sentence would lose all her marbles. She'd be living in a dream, and couldn't even notice who she was."

"She wouldn't be no different than my mom and dad," said Walter of Charlotte Street. And the whole class started to laugh, except for Tanya Greenblatt. Milo still didn't know what she was doing here. He couldn't stop gazing at her. He might lose his own marbles and disappear inside a gerund.

Dr. Muldoon was signaling to him from the door, and Milo stepped into the hall. They were confederates of a sort, the first ones in the wilderness of the South Bronx to own a Phi Beta Kappa key. Tanya Greenblatt was a special case, said Dr. Muldoon. She should have gone into an adult education program, but this school was also special, having risen out of the ruins. And since Tanya had once worked here, Dr. Muldoon had his own "legal window." She could audit Milo's classes, and Milo could become her referee.

"What kind of referee?"

"You'll tutor her in your spare time."

Milo could sniff his own destruction. He'd never survive Tanya Greenblatt. But how could he contradict a principal who had graduated from Fordham and considered the Bronx as his own fief? Dr. Muldoon had gone into the housing projects last week with half a dozen guards to rescue a student held hostage by some local drug lord. Milo had decided to come along. The dark halls and broken elevators terrified him, but he was Dr. Muldoon's good-luck charm. The drug lord had been a student of Milo's at Christopher Columbus. He wore a bandanna around his head and had one glass eye.

"Hey, Teach, you 'member me? I loved all that shit. I'm still crying over John Keats."

The hostage was let go. And Milo went back to his own little war with college admissions officers. He still performed his acrobatics in class, still danced with a piece of chalk in his fist, still hypnotized his students with tales of Byron crossing the Hellespont with his clubfoot as a rudder, but Milo himself had no rudder once Tanya stepped into his office. He wanted to knead her flesh, kiss her until her mouth was blue with mad desire.

"Ms. Greenblatt, why did you waylay Dr. Muldoon? You could have gone to another school, with students your own age."

Her broken smile ruined whatever resolve he had.

"*Waylay* is a word that's way over my head."

Milo began to mutter. "It's like lassoing someone, putting him into a corral."

"I did put him into my own corral," she said. "Why would I want to be around other wrecks my age? It would be like looking into the mirror. And I'm not blind. You're the miracle man, with your Harvard and Yale. Well, Harvard me."

"It's not that simple."

"Make it simple," she whispered.

Milo's hell began. He couldn't corral Harvard or Yale for Tanya Greenblatt. Her college boards were abysmal. There were too many gaps in her dossier. She confessed to him that she'd been a lap dancer at a downtown titty club until one of the clients broke her face. The club wouldn't help her. This crazy client had too much pull. She hired a lawyer, but someone broke his face, too. She became a nomad, like Milo, wandering from club to club, until no club would have her.

"But you had a job at this school," he said.

"And then you came along, my old flame. I couldn't bear the memories. I was fond of you at Taft."

"We barely spoke. And weren't you in love with a fireman?"

"A fireman with six wives. He lent me out to all his friends—no, I fancied you."

"I was a student teacher," Milo had to insist. "I wasn't in any shape to flirt. I'd had a kind of breakdown. I was supposed to have a university career. My mom and dad had high hopes. I won a fellowship to Oxford. I was summa cum laude."

"What's that?" she growled with a playfulness that unsettled him. He didn't have to close his eyes to imagine Tanya dancing on his lap.

"It means with the highest honors. But I couldn't really profit from it. I never became an Oxford don. My problem started at public school. I kept skipping grades until I was much too young for the students around me."

"And I'm much too old," she said. "But why didn't you kiss me once at Taft, or give me a little feel? I would have cooked for you, kept you fit. And while my fireman and his pals were poking me, I dreamt of you."

"I couldn't," Milo muttered. "I was afraid. You were such a wildflower."

"Wildflower," she whistled between the gaps in her teeth. "I like that."

Milo wanted to cry. He was already half-crazed. She kicked the door closed, held his head in her hands, and dug her lizard's tongue into his mouth. He'd never had such a kiss. And she must have had her own radar. She slid out her tongue and leapt into a chair just as Dr. Muldoon entered Milo's office.

"You'll help Ms. Greenblatt, won't you, Mr. C.?"

So he stayed with her after class, after every student was gone and there was no one but the custodian and the cook, who had to prepare next week's menu. The school's patrolmen had fixed the metal detector and returned to their precinct. And Milo had to risk his own skin. She wouldn't tell him where she lived, and she wouldn't come downtown with him to Jane Street. He had to fumble with her in that dark office. It was preposterous, with Tanya sitting on his lap while he helped her with her SATs.

I'm a retard, he told himself, *a retard in the middle of a high school romance.* Yes, yes, she'd been his old flame, the one flame he'd ever had. He worried that he might get caught in this little closet of an office. It would be the end of his career; not even his Phi Beta Kappa key could save him. But he was addicted to Tanya, and he couldn't cut it off. His students must have known. Tanya always sat in the front row, purring at him under her breath.

"Language is monstrous," he'd say, trying not to look at Tanya's legs. "Sentences are made with the Devil's own music."

"What does that mean?" asked Sheleela of Sheridan Avenue.

"Look at the way we group animals. We say a herd of elephants or an army of caterpillars. That's sensible, isn't it? But what about zebras?"

Sheleela stared at him. "Don't zebras have their herd?"

"Perhaps," said Milo. "But we still talk about a zeal of zebras, a rumba of rattlesnakes, and a shiver of sharks."

"That's cool," said Milo's brightest student, a boy from Pakistan. "A shiver of sharks."

"And there's more," said Milo. "A charm of hummingbirds, a parliament of owls, a murder of crows."

Tanya raised her hand, blinking at him with both eyelashes. "Mr. C., I can imagine owls sitting on their branch like a parliament. But why a murder of crows?"

"It must come from medieval times," he said. "You see, crows were great busybodies; they loved to perch on the ramparts of some castle and peck at the garbage. An invading army would follow these crows right into battle. And for a castle's defenders, these cawing black birds became an ominous sign, a murder of crows."

The students stared at Milo with suspicious eyes.

"That's some awesome shit," said Sheleela. "It's either brilliant or the stupidest thing I ever heard—or both."

There was a nervous ripple in class. Students could feel that curious heat in the first row. They resented Tanya and the stranglehold she seemed to have on Mr. C. Would they peck her eyes out, like a murder of crows? Would they snitch on her to Dr. Muldoon?

Milo's little world was about to crumble. He was desperate, and desperately in love. He offered to marry Tanya if she would leave his class. She cawed at him. "Not until you get me into college."

He couldn't do much with her test scores. But he knew the admissions officers at some of the smaller colleges. He helped Tanya write her college essay, where she talked about everything from purple lipstick to lap dancing. He was like a warrior attacking an enemy with his own murder of crows. He got her into a tiny college in Maine; it was the best Milo could do; Tanya would be on probation her first year, but she'd still belong to the freshman class.

She clutched the college's letter as if she were in a trance. She stopped attending Milo's class, wouldn't even sit on his lap one last time. She vanished without a word. His closet at school became a closed-in hell. All he could think about was his lap dancer. His students took pity on him. They reminded Mr. C. to comb his hair. They knew more about Tanya than he ever did. She'd been doing the rumba with Dr. Muldoon, they said. She was Muldoon's pet rattlesnake. She wore his Phi Beta Kappa key when she wasn't with Milo.

He didn't know what to believe. He wanted to run from this school. But where did he have to go? He couldn't confront Muldoon. The principal would throw him out on his ass. There were no other problem schools beyond this badland—it was the end of the line for Milo. So he martyred himself for his students. He was as ferocious and cunning as a shiver of sharks in his letters to college admissions officers. He dared the best colleges *not* to accept his students. He got one into Harvard, two into Yale.

But it was Dr. Muldoon who received most of the credit. He was the star of a PBS special about the sudden resurrection of the Bronx. Milo was only on camera for a couple of seconds. But the crew followed Dr. Muldoon into his home in Riverdale, filmed him with his wife and daughters. Milo half expected to see Tanya Greenblatt lurking behind the sofa somewhere . . .

His students were disheartened by the film. They'd cackled like crows for PBS, paid homage to Milo and Lord Byron, but their performance had been hacked to pieces.

"Where the hell was Lord Byron? We never mentioned Muldoon, and that mother was all over the place."

"Sheleela, watch your mouth," he said. "You won't be able to talk like that at Yale."

"Then Yale will have to suffer," she said.

Milo had one bit of solace. His best students came back to visit him from their college dorms. They sat with him in his closet. They kept in touch long after they graduated.

Milo even heard from Tanya Greenblatt. She scribbled a note to him from the woods of Maine.

> Dear Mr. C.,
> I was better off as your wildflower.
>
> The kids at college never liked me much. They told me I dressed like a whore. I quit school and started to work at a club in town, the Hanky-Panky. I married the manager, Mr. Forrest. I have two babies now and a shitload of relatives. My husband still has me working at the club between all the diaper brigades.
>
> You call that living? I smile when I remember that lingo you taught us about shivering sharks. I'm sorry what I did to you, sneaking behind your back with Dr. Muldoon. But why didn't you take me in your arms once

or twice when I was at William Howard Taft? I would have stuck with you, I swear it.

Faithfully yours, Mrs. Delmar Forrest
Mayflower Hill, Maine

He thought of riding a bus up to Mayflower Hill and rescuing her from the Hanky-Panky. But the police would have considered him insane—a high school teacher from the Bronx trying to tear a mother away from her brood.

He folded her letter under the green mat on his desk at school, near the gum erasers and abandoned ballpoint pens. College admissions officers phoned him several times a month, as if he were the scout of a fabulously successful franchise. But he no longer heard the voices of Byron and Keats inside his head.

ALICE'S EYES

1.

I was crazy about the old man.

He'd rescued me when I was at the home for bad boys in the Bronx. He grew up near Hunts Point, and the Bronx was still his bailiwick. He made his bundle manufacturing paper bags and buying up real estate. He had a townhouse in Greenwich Village and a horse farm near Santa Fe, but he'd become the angel of mercy at Spofford Juvenile Center.

We were sitting in the warden's office, sipping coffee from paper cups.

"What kind of name is that?" he rasped. "Ricardo Rosenwasser."

I told him. Mom was a Latin beauty and Dad was a rabbinical scholar who ran away from home. They were the Romeo and Juliet of the South Bronx . . . until they died of an overdose and I went to live with one of Dad's maiden aunts.

"Why should I help you, kid? There are a lot of juvenile offenders with a handsome IQ."

I looked that billionaire in the eye and said, "Because I'm going to save your ass."

He liked that. He was Martin Gorman, the prince of paper bags, and he called up a judge right from the warden's office. In fifteen minutes I had a brand-new fate. I was allowed to leave Spofford every morning and attend classes at the Bronx High School of Science.

And I've had a long ride on Martin Gorman's coattails ever since. I graduated cum laude from Cornell and was eleventh in my class at Harvard Law. I'm chief litigator at Burnside, Ebel & Gold, one of the most feared law firms in Manhattan. We're ruthless, and most of the ladies on a jury panel cannot resist my charm. I'm six feet two and bear an astonishing resemblance to Brad Pitt.

But all that charm hasn't been able to help the old man. He's lost his appetite. I can't even sit with him at the Four Seasons. He'll stare at his crab cakes and start to cry. He swore to me that his health was fine. So what the hell has happened?

He's been hibernating at his horse farm. I flew out to Santa Fe. I found him dozing on his verandah in the middle of the afternoon, hidden under a fancy horse blanket and a baseball cap that cost him ten grand. It had once belonged to Mickey Mantle, he said. I wanted to sue the memorabilia show that had swindled him. But he liked to dream in the Mick's old cap.

His horse farm was actually a hacienda—it covered half a dozen very brown hills. He couldn't have been much older than seventy-five, but he looked like a man in a death mask.

"Ricky, I can't eat. I can't sleep."

His butler brought me a burrito with hot sauce and a Corona in a tiny tub of ice.

"Mr. G., if it's about one of your wives, I can . . ."

"No, no, it's not matrimonial," he said. And he began to weep like a child. I wanted to take him in my arms and carry him home to Manhattan. I couldn't function amid all that mesquite and brutal sunlight.

"Whatever's wrong," I said, "I can fix it."

"Not this," he muttered. "Not this."

Now, all of sudden, he was willing to talk, and I listened to his tale. He was morose, he said, after the Bronx began to burn. "Rick, I can still feel fire on my face, and that was almost forty years ago." But it didn't prevent him from gobbling up foreclosed properties. He waited ten years until the fires died and then rebuilt in all the rubble. He hired superintendents for buildings that morphed out of the debris. But he quarreled with one of his supers, a Dominican who could do repairs in his other buildings. This super—Tiny Batista—was stealing sinks and pipes. Tiny was six-four and weighed two hundred pounds. He had a five-year-old daughter with dark eyes and would ferry her about on one shoulder, like some luxurious parrot, show her off to everyone in the barrio. And Gorman felt so betrayed, so belittled, that he decided to punish Tiny in front of his little girl. He arrived in a patrol car. The police were always escorting him around the Bronx.

"Tiny," he said, "you're a thief."

Batista was standing in front of Gorman's building on Minford Place with a coterie of friends. The crinkle had gone out of his eyes. He'd been working for Gorman ever since he was seventeen.

"Wait a second, Mr. G. I'm with my hombres. They don't have to listen . . ."

He began to paw at the prince of paper bags, playing with him like a disgruntled bear. The cops leapt from their patrol car and clubbed Tiny to the ground with their nightsticks while Gorman looked into the little girl's eyes. She wasn't sobbing. And she didn't have the fear and trembling of a child. Her brow had wrinkled up, and she seemed to mourn Mr. G. with all the sadness and wisdom of the oldest woman in the world, as if he'd broken through some boundary from which he could never return.

"But it happened years ago," I said. "Why should it suddenly start to haunt you?"

"I don't know," the horse farmer said under his fake Mickey Mantle cap.

"And what would you like me to do?"

"You'll never find her. She could be a grandma by now."

"Stop it! She can't be more than thirty-five. What was her name?"

"Little Alice."

And he was bawling again. I left him there on his verandah and caught the next flight from Santa Fe. The wizards at Burnside, Ebel & Gold punched in Orlando "Tiny" Batista, and we had a printout in five minutes. Batista was a "ghost" in their parlance. He died in 1983. Whatever wife he'd had didn't possess a Social Security number. And there was nothing on Little Alice.

"Come on, guys. A girl can't just disappear."

"Ricky, she's even more of a ghost than her old man."

But my guys uncovered a site devoted to an obscure little rag published several times a year. *Back In the Bronx.* We subscribed to the journal. I tore through every page. There was a lot about the Bronx Bombers, but nothing about a grown-up little girl from Minford Place. *Back In the Bronx* did have a classified section, which was one long lonely hearts club, with retirees in Tucson or Boca Raton looking for an old sweetie or swain. And that's where we decided to strike. I wrote the entry, like some heartless left-hander delivering his best curve.

LOOKING FOR LITTLE ALICE, DAUGHTER OF ORLANDO BATISTA, formerly of Minford Place. Prepared to pay a handsome reward. Please contact Ricardo Rosenwasser, Esq., of Burnside, Ebel & Gold. One of our clients would like to settle an old complaint. ricardo@burnside.ebel.gold.com

I coaxed Gorman back into his townhouse on Horatio Street. His malady grew worse and worse. I hired cops from the local precinct to become his babysitters, and whenever he strolled too far in his pajamas, I picked up the old man and returned him to Horatio. His skull seemed transparent when he took off his Mickey Mantle hat.

"Rick, I'll never make it. I can't stop dreaming of Alice's eyes."

I couldn't wait around for that lonely hearts column to kick in. I had to hire some desperate actress to play the grown-up Alice. I asked my junior associates to contact the most obscure talent agencies in Manhattan. Whoever auditioned was given the same spiel.

"Look," I said, "he'll cry in your arms, you'll forgive him, and you walk away with a fat check."

The auditions went on for days. Then my dream Alice walked into Burnside, Ebel & Gold like another desperate actress. But I could tell the difference. She had a kind of natural flamboyance that none of the actresses had. Her hair was swept back. Her eyes had a liquid darkness, as if pieces of black silver lay behind them. It frightened me, because she had my mother's high cheekbones and sweet arrogance.

"Sit down, please. You're not with a talent agency. You must have noticed my ad in that Bronx magazine."

"No," she said. "One of my cousins did—Orlando's oldest boy."

"I don't understand. Aren't you Tiny Batista's daughter?"

"No," she said. "I'm his niece."

"And your name isn't Alice?"

"Alicia."

I had to use whatever bit of cunning I had left. "But my client was very specific. Tiny Batista's daughter, he said."

"Tiny never had a daughter."

I offered her some coffee. We had to indulge our clients, and the firm had its own pastry chef. That was one of our signatures. I had vanilla brownies and croissants to offer Alicia. I had low-calorie shortcake. I had almond macaroons. But she would have none of our purchased plunder. She wouldn't even agree to an espresso.

"I'd rather not name my client, Alicia. But if you would agree to meet with him, I'd make it worth your while."

She laughed bitterly with those dark pieces of silver.

"Meet the worst slumlord in the Bronx? Martin Gorman had my uncle killed. I was right there. The police fed me lollipops after they finished hammering on Uncle's brains. Oh, he lived a couple of years, Mr. Rosenwasser. But I had to wheel him around. Your client paid some of the hospital bills, with Uncle's own blood."

She was beautiful with that flare of anger and bitterness, though she must have had scarlet fever as a child. I saw the pockmarks on her face.

"Your uncle did steal from him."

She reached over and tugged at my hand-painted necktie. "Ricardo, whatever Uncle stole, he stole for the slumlord."

"My client isn't a slumlord," I had to insist.

"Then what would you call a man who steals his own sinks? Tiny helped him, I admit. But the slumlord paid him a ridiculous price. And that's why they quarreled."

My voice got weaker and weaker. "How would you know all this? You were five." Alicia put two fingers into her mouth. And she whistled in such a high pitch that I thought my eardrums would shatter.

"*Five*," she said. "That was old enough to be their little accomplice. They dressed me in white, with a bridal veil. I was their lookout. They had to cart their toilet bowls and sinks away in a truck. I would stand at the corner and whirl around. If a patrol car came I would whistle . . . and flirt with the police."

It bothered me to imagine her as a little girl in a bridal veil.

"Mr. Gorman had the police in his pocket," I said.

"There were other pockets, some as huge as his own."

This beautiful Bronx witch hadn't arrived out of nowhere. I'd summoned her up via the columns of *Back In the Bronx*.

"Alicia, couldn't we have a little wine in the Village before we meet the old man? I know a diner on Hudson and Bethune—nothing fancy. It's called the Bus Stop. And it isn't far from where the old man lives."

"Shame on you," she said. "I ought to slap your fingers. Trying to hit on me. But I have no intention of meeting that slumlord again. He poisoned my childhood."

"Then why did you come here—to my office?"

"Oh," she said, "I didn't want to be impolite. And I was curious about you—a Latino lawyer in a big Jewish law firm."

"I'm half Jewish," I had to insist.

"But it's the *other* half that interested your partners. A *Borinqueño* at Burnside, Ebel & Gold."

And she walked out of my office. I didn't even know her last name. I canceled all my appointments and took a cab down to Horatio Street. Gorman wandered through his townhouse like a ghost in gray pajamas. I could barely catch up with him.

"Mr. G., slow down! I met her."

He scrutinized my face with steel in his eyes. "Little Alice?"

"Her name is Alicia. And she isn't Tiny Batista's daughter. She's his niece."

"That's impossible," the old man said. And then his mind began to recalibrate.

"Why didn't you bring her here, Rick?"

We both sat down on his stairs. "Tiny Batista wasn't your hireling. He was your partner in crime. And you had a five-year-old girl on your payroll."

"She wasn't on any payroll. We bought her outfits, dressed her up like a doll. She did a few favors for us. Why didn't you bring her here?"

"She's had enough of you for one lifetime. Was it so important to have Batista's skull bashed in?"

"He got greedy," the old man said. "He was threatening me. I thought he would back down. And then Little Alice ate me up with her eyes."

"*Alicia*," I said. And he was bawling again. He didn't even have his Mantle cap to hide his skull. There was little left of him but his eye sockets. It was a face without any flesh.

2.

I found Little Alice, even if she'd appeared in my office without a last name. My guys could track her once they knew she was Tiny's niece—Alicia Alvarez. She'd never married. She was a nurse at Montefiore Medical Center. And she must have moved away from the wild lands of Minford Place, because she lived near the hospital, at a nurses' residence on Rochambeau Avenue, in an enclave known as Norwood. It was a little golden triangle, protected from the ravages of the South Bronx by a river, a cemetery, and two parks. The Irishers had once lived there along with Jewish grocers. And I'd lived there with my maiden aunt, in a brick castle right on Rochambeau, after Mom and Dad died. I was like a scavenger in that golden triangle—I stole from stationery stores, from corner groceries, and took whatever I could find until I was put away at Spofford. I would have remained a thief if the old man hadn't waved his magic wand and gotten me into Bronx Science. So I couldn't abandon him to all the crazy wolves inside his crazy head.

But he wouldn't get dressed, not even for Alicia, and I couldn't let him walk around Rochambeau Avenue in his pajamas, like some escapee from an asylum. I had to bundle him into my overcoat. And we ventured up to Norwood in a chauffeured limousine. Auntie's brick castle was still there, with its Tudor façade, but other castles had been torn down—the medical center had gobbled up more and more space, and that golden triangle could have been Montefiore's own little garden, littered with parking lots.

We bribed a super and were able to get into Alicia's residence—it was a brick dormitory for unmarried nurses and all the other "nuns" of Montefiore. We buzzed upstairs, but Alicia wasn't home. The super lent us her key. She lived in a studio apartment that looked out onto one of the parking lots. Gorman stumbled around like a blind man, but I searched for clues. She didn't even have a bookcase—just a bare white bed, a worn sofa, a tiny kitchen with a few pots and pans, and a television set with a flat screen.

I couldn't find a hint of Alicia except for one bulletin board on a barren wall; within its wooden frame were snapshots of crippled children from Montefiore's wards—the children had wary eyes. Blue and green Post-it flags were pinned to the corkboard with little reminders of Alicia's schedule and hours. I had to decipher the scratch of her hand.

> Tell Josephine R. to meet me at six . . .
> Find Brad after his chemo . . .

Caught between the crippled children and that medley of Post-it flags was another snapshot, much older than the rest. It hung at a slant like some kind of relic in its own tiny silver frame. I wasn't stupid. I recognized Martin Gorman as a much younger man. He was standing with a giant—Tiny Batista—who had the ghostly presence of a child. There was nothing mean or malicious about the giant. He could have been a slow-witted angel. With them was the little girl who had been haunting the old man's dreams. She had chubby fingers in the photo. I could sense nothing in her face but delight—and the little signs of her scarlet fever. She was clutching Martin Gorman's ear . . .

We left the brick dormitory, and I was about to track Alicia to her station at the Children's Hospital, but I didn't have the chance. Alicia spotted us before we spotted her. She was walking on Rochambeau in a white hospital coat. Her eyebrows began to knit. It wasn't hard to read the fury on her face. She never even looked at the old man. She was staring at me with the same dark eyes that had once ripped into the old man's heart.

"I'll kill you if you ever come here again."

3.

I forgot that she had been a terrific tease when she was five, that she had flirted with strangers, wearing a child's wedding dress and a white veil, to protect the old man's toilets and sinks. When I returned to the office, I discovered an e-mail from her in my in-box.

> Ricardo, meet me tomorrow (Wednesday) at the Bus Stop, 7 P.M. sharp. Bring the slumlord. I wouldn't want him to travel too far uptown in his pajamas. He might get lost.

We arrived early and sat in one of the booths. It was a week before Halloween, and I wondered if she'd ride in on a broomstick. But Alicia showed up in a child's veil. She seemed to bloom right inside her blouse.

"Alice," the old man said, "it breaks my heart to look at you."

We were all drinking merlot.

"There's no absolution," she said, sipping from her glass.

She sat across from us. She hadn't come here to excite me and the old man, but I was excited and I shouldn't have been by some child-woman out of Martin Gorman's past. That wasn't in my playbook. But here she was, furious at the old man and me, and I was growing cockeyed as I gazed at the crook of her elbow.

"Uncle Martin," she said in a soft voice, with all the shrewdness of a little girl in a white veil. "I don't give a damn how much penance you do in your pajamas. Uncle Tiny was your partner. You shouldn't have ruined him."

"But I'll donate a million to Montefiore in *his* name. I'll endow every crippled child in the Bronx with a pair of crutches. I'll do anything you ask. Christ, I want to lie down and not have to stare at your wounded eyes in my dreams."

"But I want you to stare at them—forever."

The old man leaned over and sobbed into his salmon steak. I was the sweet-talker who could mesmerize whole juries but couldn't get back the old man's sweet dreams.

"Alicia, can't we structure a deal? One kind word would go a long way."

"Shut up," she said. "You're worse than he is. You clean up for the ghoul."

She drank more and more merlot. I'd swear she was flirting with me under her veil. I offered to drive her back to the Bronx.

"Shut up," she said. And then Alicia startled me. She reached under the veil with one finger and flicked away a tear.

"I loved to be their lookout. I'd dance in the street, while Uncle Tiny would bust his balls, carrying sinks on his back. And my other *tío*, this old man. I always danced for him, like Salome. I haven't danced ever since. Now I live . . ."

Like a monk in a closet, I muttered to myself.

She stood up, kissed the old man between the eyes with a kind of surly affection, brushed past me, and ran out of the diner. I wanted to run after her, but her *tío* grabbed me with fists that were steel bands.

"Leave her alone, Ricky. We're reconciled, and you have other fish to fry."

I couldn't move. I watched her from the window. She flew across the street in one spectacular stride—like a witch or a girl who had rediscovered dancing after a lapse of thirty years. I knew I would never see her again.

MAJOR LEAGUER

Will Johnson had been to bat five times in the big leagues. He struck out twice, botched a bunt, popped to left center, and hit into a double play, and he knew he was going back down to the Carolina League. It had something to do with the Yankee roster. There was a player in transit, and another was coming off the disabled list. So for one afternoon in 1975, he was the New York Yankees' twenty-fifth man.

What if he had gone five for five that afternoon? Would the Yankees have put that other player back in transit and kept Will on the roster? Instead, he was returned to Greensboro, where he broke his thumb in the middle of the season. That thumb never healed; it had a permanent hump. He was banished to semipro ball, and ended his career barnstorming with stumblebums. He was finished before his twenty-ninth birthday, a ballplayer with a broken hand. He drifted down to New Orleans, was a chef in Algiers until he smashed a man's collarbone in a bar fight. He ran home to the Bronx, his tail tucked between his legs.

But the Bronx seemed to be in permanent recession. His father had been an unlicensed plumber who lived in a tiny black enclave near Tremont Avenue. Will's whole family was wiped out. His father had a stroke at forty-five. His mother died of sickle-cell anemia. His baby sister bled to death during childbirth. Will's old neighborhood was in ruins. It never recovered from the highway

Robert Moses had plowed right through it. Will had met Moses as a little boy. He remembered a very tall man in a hard white hat, standing near a great hole in the ground. Moses had given Will a lollipop, had carried him in his arms.

"Son, what would you like to be when you grow up?"

Will looked into Moses' pale eyes. "A ballplayer," he said.

It was the last time he ever saw that man in his hard hat. And now Will had to scratch around for a job. A few of the old-timers remembered that he'd been in the big leagues. He was hired as a superintendent in one of the buildings that Moses hadn't managed to destroy. It was on La Fontaine Avenue, in the heart of an old Jewish quarter that had turned Latino while Will was there. Robert Moses' highway was like the avenue's own sore rib. And the heartless din of traffic from that highway had been ringing in Will's ears now for a good quarter of a century.

He was fifty-seven, with cataracts in one eye. The building on La Fontaine had stone lions in the courtyard. It had new radiators and new wiring. A renegade air conditioner couldn't sabotage its circuitry. The building was only two blocks from Quarry Road and St. Barnabas Hospital, and from time to time a nurse or a resident from St. Barnabas would move into Will's building for a while.

He'd lived with one of the nurses, a woman from the West Indies. Her name was Rosette. But she had a husband somewhere, and his brothers came looking for Will. They beat him up with a baseball bat, and he was in a coma for a month.

When he returned to La Fontaine Avenue, Rosette was gone. Will was blind in one eye after the beating. He would coach kids in the neighborhood, teach them how to bat in Tremont Park. But local gangs began to raid the park and rob these kids of their brand-new gloves. And Will wasn't going to fight a whole gang high on coca leaves. He would have landed in the hospital again.

So he kept to himself most of the time, drank in his ground-floor apartment, and earned extra money as a freelance plumber along La Fontaine.

And then she moved in. She was some kind of administrator at St. Barnabas, could have been forty years old. She had a lot of freckles. Her name was Laurencia Riley. He'd never heard a name like that. It mystified him. He repaired her toilet, began doing odd jobs for her. Will rewired one of her lamps. He wouldn't take money from her, and he wasn't sure why.

"Are you in the business of charity, Mr. Will Johnson?" she asked, without hiding her brogue. She was from Belfast, had been at a nuns' college but had never taken her vows. She was lucky enough to land a green card. She'd filed her citizenship papers, had been fingerprinted in Foley Square, but hadn't yet been asked for an interview. And she was nervous about it. "Sometimes I feel like an enemy alien."

After living in the apartment for a month, she dangled a duplicate key in front of Will. "In case you have to operate on my fridge."

"But I have the key to every apartment," Will said.

"Then be a good lad, Will Johnson, and take one from my own hand."

Her signals confused him. Laurencia wasn't like those little mamas who had followed him around while he was barnstorming with the Graystone Grasshoppers. She didn't wear midriffs and stink of perfume. But she began leaving sandwiches for him outside his apartment. And he was growing curious about her. He was a head taller than Laurencia Riley. He stood beside her like a lighthouse, a tower with one good eye.

"Why do you live here, Miss Riley?"

Most of the hospital staff and administrators lived on the far side of Fordham University, with its parks and Tudor-style apartment houses. Every street was patrolled. There were no glassine heroin bags in the gutters, with their ominous stamp of a barking, wild-eyed dog. That was the insignia of the Crotona Dogs, a street gang that had prospered while the Bronx was burning and bands of wild dogs roamed Crotona Park at will. It took years to get rid of the dogs, and meanwhile the gang morphed into the biggest distributor of heroin in the South Bronx.

That didn't seem to bother Laurencia. The no-man's-land south of Quarry Road reminded her of Belfast's bombed-out streets.

"It's where I grew up, Will, Irish fighting Irish, while the British bloodhounds sniffed at the lot of us. No, I'll stay here, thank you. Besides, you happen to live on a very poetic street."

And she told him about La Fontaine, a writer of fables who lived hundreds of years ago, before there ever was the Bronx and the wild dogs of Crotona Park. La Fontaine's favorite hero was Sir Fox, a local robber baron who preyed upon as many barnyards as he could.

"And what would Sir Fox have made of the South Bronx, Miss Riley?"

"Mr. Johnson," she said in that brogue of hers, "will you call a girl by her proper name? I'm Laurencia, for Christ's sake, or Ms. Laurencia, depending on your fancy. And Sir Fox would have thrived in this barnyard of ours, even with the Crotona Dogs, who are robbers without his etiquette and without his charm. He would have stopped their pillage, and finally he would have pilfered from them."

Will had had such poor schooling; he'd run away from home at fifteen to join a gypsy team. And here was an educated woman, a hospital administrator, who could have lived in that golden ghetto on the far side of Fordham, have met a fellow administrator or an MD and married him, yet chose the street of La Fontaine, next to a highway, with its tunnels and dead ends, where heroin addicts sought their ten-dollar bags.

"And there's another reason why I'm here, love. I happen to fancy you."

Will had never been shy before. But women with freckles and red hair always frightened him. Still, he took Laurencia Riley in his arms, and he didn't have that urge to rip her bones apart while loving her, the way he'd done with ten-dollar whores on the road. She didn't have the curves he admired, but he got to like the curves she did have. And she confessed to him that she hadn't moved here by chance. She'd seen him in the hospital while he lay in a coma.

"I couldn't take my eyes off you, love. There was a beauty in the breaths you took. Jesus, I was ashamed of myself. My own staff saw me blush, and me falling in love with a man in a coma."

"But that was two years ago."

"Will Johnson, I had to get me some courage, even if I am a spitfire with red hair. I had to be sure you weren't the Devil, trying to trick an Irish maiden."

"Well?" Will asked. "Am I the Devil?"

"Indeed. That Devil of my own."

But she wouldn't live with Will as his "common-law." They kept their own apartments, yet they found little recreation along the broken spine of Tremont Avenue. There wasn't even a movie house in the neighborhood. And she didn't thrust Will into her life at St. Barnabas. She never ate with him at one of the Italian restaurants on Arthur Avenue—Dominick's had become the hospital's own canteen. There wasn't much to explore in a no-man's-land littered with glassine bags. They discovered a few Creole restaurants near Tremont. And sometimes they'd walk up the hill to the Grand Concourse. But the Crotona Dogs had put their mark on every other wall.

The Dogs had broken up his little baseball clinic, and he couldn't complain to the cops who had deserted the badlands. The foot patrols ended near Quarry Road. Laurencia knew the South Bronx's sinister stats. It was the poorest, most crowded barrio east of the Mississippi. Harlem was a honey pot compared to the South Bronx. Will had to venture into Harlem to buy a box of blueberries.

It felt as if Robert Moses' ghost had come back again and again to haunt the neighborhoods he had ruined. The Crotona Dogs had only crept into Robert Moses' tracks and devoured what was left with their glassine bags. And Will had to play the fool and become the sheriff of his own block. He walked to the very edge of La Fontaine and swept out all the addicts who shivered in the tunnels, squatting in cardboard boxes that had become their cribs.

Laurencia understood the consequences of Will's little act better than he did. She borrowed one of the hospital's cars and they got lost for a week. They drove through Connecticut, stayed at a farm in New Hampshire near a waterfall. The sound of that water revived Will. He didn't want to go back to the Bronx. But she couldn't abandon her duties at St. Barnabas.

There were markings all over the outer wall of his building when he returned—devil dogs stamped above the windows on the ground floor. No other apartment house on La Fontaine had been touched. Laurencia wanted to go to the police.

"Love," she said, "we're a hospital. We have good relations with the precinct. Detectives are in our corridors all the time."

"No cops," he said. "They'll come to the hospital in their polished shoes. But they can't protect us."

"Then what should we do, Will?"

"Negotiate."

She loved this madman she was with, and she worried about him. But Will didn't have to wait. The Dogs wouldn't descend upon La Fontaine with their machine pistols and firebombs. The Bronx had stopped burning twenty years ago. A limousine parked in front of the building. A lawyer stepped onto the curb. He had all the sleek lines of Manhattan about him. He knocked on Will's door and introduced himself as the gang's own lawyer. His name was Marcus. He handed Will a bankbook with a pig-skin cover.

"We opened it at West Fork Mutual. It used to be affiliated with the Bowery Savings Bank. We thought you'd appreciate the gesture, considering that Joe DiMaggio was once a pitchman for the Bowery. . . . Will, have a look."

The account was in Will's name. There was one entry inside for three thousand dollars.

"They don't do bankbooks anymore, Will. It's wasteful and old-fashioned. But the manager's a friend of mine, and I told him it was a special case."

Will's bad eye began to quiver. "Mr. Marcus," he said, "please stop the fancy footwork. What's this for?"

"Your first payment for policing the 'hood."

"I don't get it. I kicked some addicts out of a tunnel near the highway."

"Ah, but they weren't *our* addicts. They were using a rival product. They'd bought on the cheap—from Monster Man. The worst kind of stuff."

"But that was only an accident," Will said. "I would have done the same thing if their baggies had come from the Dogs."

"We're cleaning up the 'hood. You won't find our baggies within a half mile of any public school in the barrio."

"I still can't accept your three thousand dollars."

"Ah, then that's a pity," the lawyer said. He removed a hand cannon from his briefcase. "Don't be alarmed, Will. The gun is for my own protection."

"Why would I want to harm you?"

"We have three men outside St. Barnabas prepared to torch the place. And unless you get off your sorry black ass and come with me, St. Barnabas will fare no better than a burning barn . . . and you might lose that missus of yours, the Mick with a poetic name."

He knew it would happen one day; he couldn't avoid the New York Yankees for the rest of his life. But he didn't have to enter that morgue of the old Yankee Stadium. How many times had he read about the new stadium, a monument to the twenty-first-century Yanks, with enormous murals of A-Rod & Company on the outer wall? And so he didn't protest when the Dogs' own lawyer let him out of his limo at a side gate; he didn't have to march in with the crowd. He was waltzed right through by an attendant, and rode on a tiny elevator that made a wondrous, whistling sound. It was like a fable out of La Fontaine.

He ended up in some damn box that leaned over the field like a crazy cliff. Will had never seen anything like it in all his travels as a barnstormer with the Grasshoppers. Waiters were flocking around a man with a silver ring in one ear. He looked like a Nuyorican nigger. But Will recognized who he was: Roberto Collins, the head dog of the Crotona Dogs. Will had seen his picture in the *Post*.

Roberto Collins had survived a hundred gang wars; he had a deep scar on his left cheek. He couldn't have been much older than thirty. He hadn't started the Dogs, but had risen through the ranks as a street warrior.

"Hey, homey," he said. "Sit down and enjoy the game."

Will resisted all the mechanics and rituals of Yankee baseball.

He didn't want to watch A-Rod and Jeter, but he did. The field unfolded under him like a glittering green carpet.

"You're my hero," Roberto Collins said.

"Mr. Collins, I'm a superintendent of an apartment house with a crumbling courtyard. One day a kid will disappear in the rubble."

"Means nothing. You're a New York Yankee."

"I played in one game. I struck out twice. I couldn't buy a base hit. I shouldn't have been brought up. It was an accountant's error. They needed a twenty-fifth man while another Yankee was in transit."

"Ah, but my pappy saw you. A kid from the Bronx. That's what the announcer called you—'a home-grown product.' Pappy remembered those words."

But Will remembered nothing quite so grand. He'd been a transient, a single-day wonder.

"How many homeys got to wear that uniform, huh? I grew up under a pile of shit near Crotona Park. I saw those fucking dogs chew up a child. That's how the gang began. We had to retake our territories from a gang of wild dogs. We had fatalities; a couple of us died of blood poisoning. I was a baby at the time. I couldn't do much. But Pappy kept saying over and over, 'Star-r-r-r-ting in center field, Will Johnson of the Bronx.' That was my mantra."

"I won't steal for you, Mr. Collins. I won't beat up addicts, no matter what brand name they have on their baggies. And I won't take your money."

"It's not that simple. But you're right. We are a brand name. And we have to protect that brand. We've built a farmers' market, right on Hoe Avenue. We give stipends to junior high school students. . . . I can't take back that three thousand. It'll look bad. How will I keep the cops under control if I can't control one super in my territories? You can piss the money away. That won't bother me. But you're getting three thousand a month."

Roberto Collins left after the seventh inning. Will watched Jeter go to his left and make an underhanded lob to first. After that he fled Yankee Stadium. He should have told Laurencia about the bankbook, but he didn't. Stonemasons arrived one afternoon and repaired the crumbling courtyard. These masons also worked at Woodlawn Cemetery. The managing agent for the apartment house was never presented with a bill. Statements arrived every month from West Fork Mutual like clockwork. Will was always three thousand dollars richer than the month before.

He hid the statements and the bankbook. Some boys' club called and asked him to coach a sandlot team in Crotona Park. How could Will refuse a bunch of little homeys? He knew it was the Dogs' own team. But he could heal the wound of that one wounded day at Yankee Stadium by helping these sandlotters hit, field, and run.

Will's picture was in the *Post*. He was called an ex–Yankee slugger. He was asked to speak at local churches and a synagogue in Riverdale. Soon he was listed as one of the borough's "Hundred Top Shakers." He still hadn't told Laurencia about the bankbook. And then, that fall, after the sandlotters' season, several Homeland Security agents broke into Laurencia's apartment in the middle of the night while Will was sleeping there. These agents didn't say a word to him. They identified themselves, asked to see Laurencia's green card, told her to get dressed, and spirited her away.

Will didn't know what to do. He'd never dealt with immigration lawyers, or lawyers of any kind, except Marcus, the Dogs' own man. He called Marcus at three in the morning and left a barely comprehensible message. Will's phone rang five minutes later. Roberto Collins was on the line.

"I heard all about it, homey. We'll get your missus back."

Laurencia was home an hour or two after sunrise. She wouldn't allow Will to take her in his arms.

"Jesus, why didn't you tell me you worked for the Crotona Dogs? I might have been prepared, Will. I might have known what to say."

"It was a baseball team," he whispered.

"The Dogs' own team, and you with a bankbook from them that lists me as the beneficiary."

"I didn't know that," he said.

"Then what do you know, Will?"

She started to cry. "Couldn't you have seen the nose in front of your face? Are you that much of a child? I'll never become a citizen now."

She didn't lose her job. The hospital was frightened of a lawsuit. So it kept her on the payroll and relieved her of all responsibilities. Then it offered to buy out her contract. It was some kind of silver parachute. She was branded, a maiden of forty who'd never find another job in hospital administration. Her eyes began to flutter. She cringed whenever Will went near her. She started to cry and never seemed to stop. She accepted that silver parachute.

"I can't stay here, Will. I'm sorry. I still love you, but I can't stay."

She packed some summer clothes in one tiny suitcase, as if she were leaving for a weekend. She caressed the little scar above his right eye—a baseball wound—and walked out of La Fontaine Avenue. She'd left most of her belongings behind. Will fondled every skirt and blouse and moved them into his own apartment.

Six months passed. He shambled about like some casualty of war. He stopped doing repairs, started mumbling to himself. And then that lawyer man, Marcus of Manhattan, knocked on his door.

"Come with me."

They rode in the lawyer's limousine, right on Robert Moses' highway, and ended up in Darien, Connecticut.

"Roberto had me find the missus for you. She was working as a housekeeper."

Will mulled that word in his head. "Housekeeper? That's impossible, man. She has an education. She knows all about fables and talking foxes. She had a staff of twenty under her at St. Barnabas."

"Super, she swallowed a whole bottle of pills."

They parked outside a tiny hospital near a bone-dry riverbed. It was the Dogs' own lawyer who got Will inside, who listed him as her next of kin. She had her own room. Will sat near Laurencia, clutched her hand. She'd waken, look at him, close her eyes again.

A car drove him up to Connecticut every other morning. He sat with her into the night, when all visitors had to leave. The freckles seemed to have fled from her face. She smiled at him during his third visit. His shoulders started to shake.

"Stop that, Will," she said. Those were the first words she had uttered from her bed. "Your shoulders will disappear from all that shivering."

She giggled like a little girl. But her laughing fit didn't last. And Will was mortified by that absence of freckles.

"I ruined your life. And it's all on account of a bankbook I never asked for and never used."

"Will, Will," she said. "You spent too much time with your Grasshoppers—a barnstorming baby. You fathered yourself, Will Johnson. It's a miracle. That's what I first saw in your face when you were lying there at St. Barnabas, the longest man-child in creation. Jesus, your feet were too big for the bed."

And now both of them laughed. And that very night, after he returned from Connecticut, another limousine appeared on La Fontaine. The window opened with the force of a pile driver. Roberto Collins sat inside.

"Homey, we didn't mean to harm you. We needed a touch of respectability."

"That's a laugh. I was a Yankee for one lousy afternoon."

"Don't say that, dog. A Bronx Bomber is a Bomber for life. My pappy loved you until he died."

"I wish he had never seen me play," Will said.

The window shut with the very same force. And Roberto Collins rode back into the night. A messenger delivered a packet to Will in the morning. He found a letter inside from the manager at West Fork Mutual. His account at the bank had been opened by mistake. The money wasn't Will's. The account was null and void. And the manager asked Will to tear up the bankbook and every other trace of that "renegade account," as he called it.

An ambulance arrived that afternoon from Darien. Laurencia climbed out with the help of a cane and rambled across the courtyard on her own. She had to stay with Will. Her own apartment had been rented out months ago.

"Don't get any ideas, Will. It's just for now," she said, smiling at his enormous form. "After all, you are my next of kin. The hospital got a real kick out of that. That's some lawyer you have, love. You were listed as my half brother."

He took care of Laurencia, fed her, washed her clothes. And then all manner of strangeness arrived, as if La Fontaine were visiting his own avenue of fables. Laurencia received a registered letter from St. Barnabas, in care of Will. The hospital's director apologized. There had been an error of mistaken identity. And he was abiding by the wishes of Laurencia's attorney—she had no attorney. The hospital had agreed to rehire her. In fact, her employment had never been terminated, he said. The hospital had been "maliciously misinformed." The bank account in question, of which she was the beneficiary, was the product of someone's willful imagination.

She received another letter in care of Will—from the U.S. Citizenship and Immigration Services, reminding Laurencia that her naturalization interview had been scheduled for next month. It was as if that early morning raid by Homeland Security had never happened.

She settled in with Will. He slept in the living room, on a sofa, and tucked her in at night. Her freckles had come back. "Mr. Will Johnson," she whispered, "are you Sir Fox looking far and wide for some grapes?"

"The grapes are right here," he whispered right back while she pulled apart the covers and invited him into his own bed. She wasn't shy with him that night. And she brought him to Dominick's the next day, St. Barnabas' own canteen. Will was wearing a Hawaiian shirt. He had the lean look of a barnstormer.

No synagogue or church asked him to speak about his short life as a major leaguer. The glassine bags disappeared from La Fontaine Avenue. The barnstormer was never bothered again.

WHITE TRASH

Prudence had escaped from the women's farm in Milledgeville and gone on a crimefest. She murdered six men and a woman, robbed nine McDonald's and seven Home Depots in different states. She wore a neckerchief gathered under her eyes and carried a silver Colt that was more like an heirloom than a good, reliable gun. The Colt had exploded in her face during one of the robberies at McDonald's, but she still managed to collect the cash, and her own willfulness wouldn't allow her to get a new gun.

She wasn't willful about one thing: she never used a partner, male or female.

Women were more reliable than men; they wouldn't steal your money and expect you to perform sexual feats with their friends. But women thieves could be just as annoying. She'd had her fill of them at the farm, where they read her diary and borrowed her books. Pru didn't appreciate big fat fingers touching her personal library. Readers were like pilgrims who had to go on their own pilgrimage. Pru was a pilgrim, or at least that's what she imagined. She read from morning to night whenever she wasn't out foraging for hard cash. One of her foster mothers had been a relentless reader, and Prudence had gone right through her shelves, book after book: biographies, Bibles, novels, a book on building terrariums, a history of photography, a history of dance, and *Leonard*

Maltin's Movie Guide, which she liked the best, because she could read the little encapsulated portraits of films without having to bother about the films themselves. But she lost her library when she broke out of jail, and it bothered her to live without books.

The cops had caught on to her tactics, and her picture was nailed to the wall inside post offices, supermarkets, and convenience stores; she might have been trapped in a Home Depot outside Savannah if she hadn't noticed a state trooper fidgeting with his hat while he stared at her face on the wall.

Pru had to disappear or she wouldn't survive her next excursion to Home Depot or McDonald's. And no book could help her now. Travel guides couldn't map out some no-man's-land where she might be safe. But Emma Mae, her cellmate at Milledgeville, had told her about a particular casbah called the Bronx where the cops never patrolled McDonald's. Besides, she hadn't murdered a single soul within five hundred miles of Manhattan or the Bronx. Pru wasn't a mad dog, as the bulletins had labeled her. She had to shoot the night manager at each McDonald's, because that would paralyze the customers and discourage anyone from coming after her.

She got on a Greyhound wearing eyeglasses and a man's lumber jacket after cutting her hair in the mirror of a public toilet. She'd been on the run for two months. Crime wasn't much of a business. Murdering people, and she still had to live from hand to mouth.

She couldn't remember how she landed in the Bronx. She walked up the stairs of a subway station, saw a synagogue that had been transformed into a Pentecostal church, then a building with a mural on its back wall that pictured a paradise with crocodiles, palm trees, and a little girl. The Bronx was filled with Latinas and burly black men, Emma Mae had told her; the only whites who lived there were "trash"—outcasts and country people who had to relocate. Pru could hide among them, practically invisible in a casbah that no one cared about.

Emma Mae had given her an address, a street called Marcy Place, where the cousin of a cousin lived, a preacher who played the tambourine and bilked white trash, like Prudence and Emma. He was right at the door when Pru arrived, an anemic-looking man dressed in black, with the same white streak in his hair that some skunks seemed to have, but he didn't have a skunk's eyes; his were clear as pale green crystals that burned right into Pru. She was hypnotized without his having to say a single syllable. He laughed at her disguise, and that laughter seemed to break the spell.

"Prudence Miller," he said, "are you a man or a girl?"

His voice was reedy, much less potent than his eyes.

Emma Mae must have told him about her pilgrimage to the Bronx. But Pru still didn't understand what it meant to be the cousin of a cousin. His name was Omar Kaplan. It must have been the alias of an alias, since Omar couldn't have been a Christian name. She'd heard all about Omar Khayyám, the Persian philosopher and poet who was responsible for the *Rubaiyat*, the longest love poem in history, though she hadn't read a line. And this Omar must have been a philosopher as well as a fraud—his apartment, which faced a brick wall, was lined with books. He had all the old Modern Library classics, like *Anna Karenina* and *The Brothers Karamazov*, books that Pru had discovered in secondhand shops in towns that had a college campus.

"You'll stay away from McDonald's," he said in that reedy voice of his, "and you'd better not have a gun."

"Then how will I earn my keep, Mr. Omar Kaplan? I'm down to my last dollar."

"Consider this a religious retreat or a rest cure, but no guns. I'll stake you to whatever you need."

Pru laughed bitterly but kept that laugh locked inside her throat. Omar Kaplan intended to turn her into a slave, to write his own *Rubaiyat* on the softest parts of her flesh. She waited for him to pounce. He didn't touch her or steal her gun. She slept with the silver Colt under her pillow, on a cot near the kitchen, while Omar had the bedroom all to himself. It was dark as a cave. He'd emerge from the bedroom, dressed in black, like some Satan with piercing green eyes, prepared to soft-soap whatever white trash had wandered into the Bronx. He'd leave the apartment at seven in the morning and wouldn't return before nine at night. But there was always food in the fridge, fancier food than she'd ever had: salmon cutlets, Belgian beer, artichokes, strawberries from Israel, a small wheel of Swiss cheese with blue numbers stamped on the rind.

He was much more talkative after he returned from one of his pilferings. He'd switch off all the lamps and light a candle, and they'd have salmon cutlets together, drink Belgian beer. He'd rattle his tambourine from time to time, sing Christian songs. It could have been the dark beer that greased his tongue.

"Prudence, did you ever feel any remorse after killing those night managers?"

"None that I know of," she said.

"Their faces don't come back to haunt you in your dreams?"

"I never dream," she said.

"Do you ever consider all the orphans and widows you made?"

"I'm an orphan," she said, "and maybe I just widened the franchise."

"Pru the orphan maker."

"Something like that," she said.

"Would you light a candle with me for their lost souls?"

She didn't care. She lit the candle, while Satan crinkled his eyes and mumbled something. Then he marched into his bedroom and closed the door. It galled her. She'd have felt more comfortable if he'd tried to undress her. She might have slept with Satan, left marks on his neck.

She would take long walks in the Bronx, with her silver gun. She sought replicas of herself, wanderers with pink skin. But she found Latinas with baby carriages, old black women outside a beauty parlor, black and Latino men on a basketball court. She wasn't going to wear a neckerchief mask and rob men and boys playing ball.

The corner she liked best was at Sheridan Avenue and East 169th, because it was a valley with hills on three sides, with bodegas and other crumbling little stores, a barbershop without a barber, apartment houses with broken courtyards and rotting steel gates. The Bronx was a casbah, like Emma Mae had said, and Pru could explore the hills that rose up around her, that seemed to give her some sort of protective shield. She could forget about Satan and silver guns.

She returned to Marcy Place. It was long after nine, and Omar Kaplan hadn't come home. She decided to set the table, prepare a meal of strawberries, Swiss cheese, and Belgian beer. She lit a candle, waiting for Omar. She grew restless, decided to read a book. She swiped *Sister Carrie* off the shelves—a folded slip of paper fell out, some kind of impromptu bookmark. But this bookmark had her face on it, and a list of her crimes. It had a black banner on top. WANTED DEAD OR ALIVE. Like the title of a macabre song. There were words scribbled near the bottom: "Dangerous and demented." Then scribbles in another hand: "A real prize package. McDonald's ought to give us a thousand free Egg McMuffins for this fucking lady." Then a signature that could have been a camel's hump. The letters on that hump were "O-M-A-R."

She shouldn't have stayed another minute. But she had to tease out the logic of it all. Emma Mae had given her a Judas kiss, sold her to some supercop. Why hadn't Satan arrested her the second she'd opened the door? He was toying with her like an animal trainer who would point her toward McDonald's, where other supercops were waiting with closed-circuit television cameras. They meant to film her at the scene of the crime, so she could act out some unholy procession that would reappear on the six o'clock news.

A key turned in the lock. Pru clutched her silver Colt. Omar appeared in dark glasses that hid his eyes. He wasn't dressed like a lowlife preacher man. He wore a silk tie and a herringbone suit. He wasn't even startled to see a gun in his face. He smiled and wouldn't beg her not to shoot. It should have been easy. He couldn't put a spell on her without his pale green eyes.

"White trash," she said. "Is Emma Mae your sister?"

"I have a lot of sisters," he said, still smiling.

"And you're a supercop and a smarty-pants."

"Me? I'm the lowest of the low. A freelancer tied to ten different agencies, an undercover kid banished to the Bronx. Why didn't you run? I gave you a chance. I left notes for you in half my books, a hundred fucking clues."

"Yeah, I'm Miss Egg McMuffin. I do McDonald's. And I have no place to run to. Preacher man, play your tambourine and sing your last song."

She caught a glimpse of the snub-nosed gun that rose out of a holster she hadn't seen. She didn't even hear the shot. She felt a thump in her chest and she flew against the wall with blood in her eyes. And that's when she had a vision of the night managers behind all the blood. Six men and a woman wearing a McDonald's bib, though she hadn't remembered them wearing bibs at all. They had eye sockets without the liquid complication of eyes themselves. Pru was still implacable toward the managers. She would have shot them all over again. But she did sigh once before the night managers disappeared and she fell into Omar Kaplan's arms like a sleepy child.

ABOUT THE AUTHOR

Jerome Charyn has received the Rosenthal Award in Fiction from the American Academy of Arts and Letters and was a finalist for the PEN/Faulkner Award. He was named a Commander of Arts and Letters by the French minister of culture in 2002. His stories have appeared in *The Atlantic*, *The Paris Review*, *Narrative*, *The American Scholar*, *StoryQuarterly*, and other magazines. His most recent novel was *I Am Abraham*, published by Liveright. He lives in New York.